"Let's Live Dangerously,"

Deck said.

Silver shook her head. "Sorry. I've had my share of danger. I'm looking for safe and comfortable these days."

His mouth thinned to a flat line. "I haven't felt *comfortable* since the day you bumped into me in the grocery store. I can guarantee you that you and I aren't going to be *comfortable* together." His lips tilted into a sideways smile. "At least not until we're both too exhausted to move."

His words brought mental images she'd rather not have slipping through her mind. Did he have any idea how badly she wanted him?

Probably, she decided, noting the glint in his eye.

"As for *safe*," he said, "isn't it better to take a chance sometimes when the reward might be worth it?"

Dear Reader,

This April of our 20th anniversary year, Silhouette will continue to shower you with powerful, passionate, provocative love stories!

Cait London offers an irresistible MAN OF THE MONTH, *Last Dance,* which also launches her brand-new miniseries FREEDOM VALLEY. Sparks fly when a strong woman tries to fight her feelings for the rugged man who's returned from her past. *Night Music* is another winner from BJ James's popular BLACK WATCH series. Read this touching story about two wounded souls who find redeeming love in each other's arms.

Anne Marie Winston returns to Desire with her emotionally provocative *Seduction, Cowboy Style,* about an alpha male cowboy who seeks revenge by seducing his enemy's sister. In *The Barons of Texas: Jill* by Fayrene Preston, THE BARONS OF TEXAS miniseries offers another feisty sister, and the sexy Texan who claims her.

Desire's theme promotion THE BABY BANK, in which interesting events occur on the way to the sperm bank, continues with Katherine Garbera's *Her Baby's Father.* And Barbara McCauley's scandalously sexy miniseries SECRETS! offers another tantalizing tale with *Callan's Proposition,* featuring a boss who masquerades as his secretary's fiancé.

Please join in the celebration of Silhouette's 20th anniversary by indulging in all six Desire titles—which will fulfill *your* every desire!

Enjoy!

Joan Marlow Golan

Joan Marlow Golan
Senior Editor, Silhouette Desire

Please address questions and book requests to:
Silhouette Reader Service
U.S.: 3010 Walden Ave., P.O. Box 1325, Buffalo, NY 14269
Canadian: P.O. Box 609, Fort Erie, Ont. L2A 5X3

Seduction,
Cowboy Style
ANNE MARIE WINSTON

Published by Silhouette Books

America's Publisher of Contemporary Romance

For Kathy Bostic,
great pal and traveling companion extraordinaire…
But next time I'll read the map, Thelma.
And
With special thanks to Richard and Kathy Jobgen
of Kadoka, South Dakota, for their hospitality and
unending patience with idiotic lady tourists.

 SILHOUETTE BOOKS

ISBN 0-373-76287-9

SEDUCTION, COWBOY STYLE

Books by Anne Marie Winston

Silhouette Desire

*Butler County Brides

ANNE MARIE WINSTON

has believed in happy endings all her life. Having the opportunity to share them with her readers gives her great joy. Anne Marie enjoys figure skating and working in the gardens of her south-central Pennsylvania home.

IT'S OUR 20ᵗʰ ANNIVERSARY!
We'll be celebrating all year,
Continuing with these fabulous titles,
On sale in April 2000.

Romance

#1438 Carried Away
Kasey Michaels/Joan Hohl

#1439 An Eligible Stranger
Tracy Sinclair

#1440 A Royal Marriage
Cara Colter

VIRGIN BRIDES

#1441 His Wild Young Bride
Donna Clayton

#1442 At the Billionaire's Bidding
Myrna Mackenzie

#1443 The Marriage Badge
Sharon De Vita

Desire

#1285 Last Dance
Cait London

#1286 Night Music
BJ James

#1287 Seduction, Cowboy Style
Anne Marie Winston

#1288 The Barons of Texas: Jill
Fayrene Preston

#1289 Her Baby's Father
Katherine Garbera

SECRETS! **#1290 Callan's Proposition**
Barbara McCauley

Intimate Moments

#997 The Wildes of Wyoming—Hazard
Ruth Langan

#998 Daddy by Choice
Paula Detmer Riggs

#999 The Harder They Fall
Merline Lovelace

#1000 Angel Meets the Badman
Maggie Shayne

#1001 Cinderella and the Spy
Sally Tyler Hayes

#1002 Safe in His Arms
Christine Scott

Special Edition

#1315 Beginning with Baby
Christie Ridgway

#1316 The Sheik's Kidnapped Bride
Susan Mallery

#1317 Make Way for Babies!
Laurie Paige

#1318 Surprise Partners
Gina Wilkins

#1319 Her Wildest Wedding Dreams
Celeste Hamilton

#1320 Soul Mates
Carol Finch

One

"**H**ey, hold up."

Deck Stryker ambled after his brother Marty, who had just grabbed a grocery cart and headed off down an aisle. It was hard to get lost in the only grocery store in Kadoka, South Dakota, but by the time he got to the corner, Marty had vanished.

Dammit, there was no need to act like he was going to a fire. Striding forward at a faster pace, Deck passed one empty aisle and turned down another—

And banged smack into somebody coming the other way. In the milliseconds that it took his brain to react to the impact, his senses registered softness, full breasts that flattened momentarily against his chest, and a faint floral scent that teased his nose. A woman.

Automatically he reached out, his hands circling her waist as she pitched sideways and staggered to regain her balance. A box of noodles she'd been carrying bounced out of her arms and skittered across the floor, and Deck put out a boot to stop it.

Releasing the woman, he bent and retrieved the box, then straightened and offered it to her. ''Sorry, ma'am.''

''I'm sorry, too,'' she said, ''I wasn't paying attention...'' She broke off and stared up at him, and for a moment, all he could do was stare back.

Attraction. Hot, instinctive awareness, the kind that crashed over a man and left him gasping for air, hit him full in the face. He knew her without ever seeing her before, recognized her, was drawn to her.

Her eyes were compelling, an odd shade of silvery-gray, their thick, dark lashes accenting the softness into which he fell. Deep in his gut, arousal woke as suddenly as if he'd been yanked from sleep by a loud alarm. His fingers tingled where he'd held her waist as if they would carry the imprint of her forever.

She wasn't a short woman. In the instant in which momentum had plastered her against him her eyes had been level with his mouth. And her body... She'd felt delicate beneath his hands, fine-boned and fragile. As he ran his gaze down over the rest of her, his mind gave a silent wolf whistle. *Long and lean* were the first words that came to mind. But not too lean, he thought, measuring with his eyes the soft mounds of her breasts pushing at the lavender knit shirt she wore. She had a jean jacket tied around her slender waist which she'd probably discarded when the cool May morning turned into an uncomfortably warm afternoon.

With the shirt, she wore totally impractical, white, city-girl jeans. It confirmed his initial thought that she wasn't a local girl. The shirt set off her fair ivory skin so that it held a translucent glow and made her eyes seem incredibly striking. Molten silver encased in those dark lashes.

He'd never seen eyes like that. They slanted up slightly at the corners, giving her the look of an exotic cat.

She had a strong-boned face with arching dark eyebrows. Dark hair so brown it looked nearly black was caught back from her high forehead with a hair band from which it curled in wild corkscrews to her shoulderblades. Her nose was straight and slim, her cheekbones high and broad, and her mouth… As his gaze skimmed over the full bottom lip and the curved bow of her upper one, the arousal simmering beneath his skin heated up another degree or two.

Abruptly he realized he was staring. That she was staring right back seemed beside the point. She probably wondered if he was crazy.

"I was looking for someone," he told her. "I apologize again, ma'am."

"No harm done. I'm not hurt." She smiled at him, and the mental wolf whistle died away to a whimper of pure, unadulterated lust. Her mouth was too wide. It should have looked odd, but combined with the rest of her features it only gave her an incredibly sexy, pouty look in repose. When she smiled, her lips parted to reveal perfect teeth and her eyes acquired a distinctly devilish gleam.

"Good." He wondered what else he should say, but talking wasn't what he did best. Finally he simply tipped his hat and stepped to one side.

Those unusual eyes clung to his for a moment more, but after a short hesitation she stepped past him and went on around the corner from which he'd just come.

When she disappeared around the corner, Deck had to curb the urge to snatch her back. Slowly he started forward again, continuing on through the tiny store. Who was she? Jackson County barely had a thousand people running around it. Surely he'd have heard about it, if a woman who looked like that had been here for long.

"Ready to go?" His brother appeared, pushing a cart toward the checkout counter. He stopped, eyeing Deck warily. "What's the matter?"

"Nothing." He made an effort to focus, pushing a too-wide, too-kissable mouth from his mind. "Did you get cereal?"

Marty indicated the cart, which contained several boxes of the food Deck considered an essential. "Sometimes I feel like your wife," he said in disgust.

Deck only half registered the comment. He scanned the front of the store, then looked back down the aisles in his line of sight, searching for quirky black curls and long, long legs. But he didn't see her the entire time he tossed the contents of the cart onto the counter.

Her heart-shaped face was still in his mind as they exited the store, each man carrying two bags of groceries.

"Seventy bucks!" Marty complained. "Seventy dollars and all we get are four lousy little bags of groceries. I didn't even buy any meat except for hot dogs."

Deck ignored him.

"Can you believe it?" Marty went on as they walked to Deck's black Ford pickup parked in an angled space along Main Street in front of the store. "The price of— *holy smokes, will you look at that?*"

Deck lifted his head from the bags he was stashing in the back of the truck. He looked in the direction Marty was staring...and there she was.

"Now *that's* a goddess," said his brother in a reverent tone.

Deck had to agree, although he didn't like the way his brother was eyeing her. Then again, how many men would ignore her? Silver Eyes must have come out of the store a little bit ahead of them, because there she was, standing uncertainly along the curb a little way down the street. Although he was too far away to see her face clearly, her body language looked anxious and unsettled as she scanned the long, wide-open street as if she was waiting for someone who hadn't shown up.

"Quick," said Marty. "Get in. She might need a ride."

But before either of them could act on the words, a brand-new pickup turned the corner down by the city bar and slowed to a stop in front of the store. Silver Eyes set the single bag she carried in the bed and climbed into the cab. As she opened the passenger-side door and slid in, the man in the driver's seat looked up and the late-afternoon sunlight fell full on his face.

Deck heard the startled curse his brother muttered. He was too shocked to say anything at all.

The man driving away with Silver Eyes was Cal McCall.

He couldn't believe it.

The next morning, as Deck manhandled a laden wheelbarrow from the barn to the manure pile, he still hadn't shaken the image of the silver-eyed woman with whom he'd collided in the grocery story. Of all the cussed, lousy luck in the world, why did she have to be McCall's woman? The man didn't deserve to have a good dog, let alone a fine-looking woman like that.

He gritted his teeth as he emptied the wheelbarrow and started back toward the barn. Damn that low-life, cowardly bastard! What was he doing back in Kadoka after thirteen years? Nobody thought he'd ever come back.

And if he had any decency in him at all, he wouldn't.

It wasn't as if Deck needed a reminder of the night Genie had died. Genie—his twin sister, frozen in the town's memory at the age of sixteen. The hair shirt of guilt he'd worn ever since ensured that his memory stay razor sharp and crystal clear.

They'd gone to a community dance. Marty had driven separately, since he and Lora Emerson were a serious item and he'd wanted privacy from his kid sister and brother, the "terrible twinnibles" as he'd called them since they were old enough to toddle around after him. Although they both had driver's licenses, they decided to ride into the auditorium with the brothers' best friend, Cal McCall, whose family owned the next ranch over. He could still remember waving goodbye to his dad who'd stood on the porch watching as they'd bounced out the lane.

See you. We'll be back before dawn.

They'd all thought that was hilarious. And so were the raunchy lyrics of the song they'd sung on the way into town until Genie had balled her fists and hit each of them in the shoulder hard enough to leave a bruise.

Just before eleven Cal and Elmer Drucker had gotten into a fight. They'd been fooling around all evening, vying for the attention of the same girl, and when she'd danced two dances in a row with Elmer, Cal had started a little ruckus. The little ruckus turned into a roll-around-on-the-floor wrestling match until a couple of other guys pulled them apart. Elmer had a cut above his eyebrow that needed stitches so his older brother took him on over to wake up the doctor.

See you. Don't let him stitch your eye shut.

Cal had strutted around like a banty rooster—until his knee had swollen to the size of a cantaloupe and he'd had to admit he wrenched it pretty good. He'd sat in the corner with ice on it for a while and let the girls fuss over him, but eventually he'd crooked a finger at Deck. "This thing hurts. I think I'd better get home and rub some of that horse liniment on it. We're branding tomorrow and Dad'll kick my butt if I can't ride. You ready?''

It would haunt Deck forever to know that if he'd answered that question differently, his sister might be alive today.

But at the time, he'd thought he had a pretty good chance of finding out whether those enormous jugs under Andrea Stinsen's shirt were real, so when he saw Cal limping his way, he'd been all too ready to agree when Genie volunteered to take him home.

See you. I'll catch a ride with Marty later.

It was just his luck that less than fifteen minutes later, Marty was beckoning. How the heck was a guy supposed to score when he kept being interrupted? But he hadn't been that unhappy. It was apparent by then that pretty Andrea had no intention of letting him check out the contents of her bra that night, so after one last sloppy, steamy adolescent kiss Deck had headed home with Marty.

See you. I'll come by tomorrow.

But they'd only been halfway down the highway when he saw the flashing lights. Marty had skidded to a panicked stop, recognizing the overturned vehicle as Cal's father's pickup...the truck Cal had been driving. Deck was out of the truck before it fully stopped. Emergency workers were already there, and until he explained who he was, they wouldn't let him into the ambulance that was getting ready to pull away. A part of him registered the enormous hulk of a dead steer in the road, another part noted Cal talking and gesturing as he lay on an additional stretcher being loaded into the second ambulance. But he'd been too frantic about Genie to care about anything else.

She was still conscious when he'd climbed into the back of the ambulance. He wouldn't have known her if it weren't for the blue chambray shirt she'd been wearing and the silver buckle she'd won barrel racing that decorated her belt. God, *the blood.* He'd seen a lot of blood in his work on the ranch but he hoped he never saw anything like that again.

Her eyes had been closed and she'd been moaning in pain, but when he took her hand and spoke to her, she'd whispered, "Deck."

He hadn't been able to speak for the fear that clutched his throat, so he bent his head and kissed her fingers.

She'd stirred and opened the one eye that wasn't swollen shut. "Don't blame Cal."

Don't blame Cal.

She'd never spoken again.

Marty had gone on home to tell their parents, while Deck rode to Rapid City in the ambulance with his unconscious twin. Twelve hours later she'd died in the hospital without ever knowing that her family was around her, without ever knowing that the man who'd done this to her was lounging in a hospital bed up in Philip with a few broken bones instead of in a jail cell where Deck wanted to see him.

See you…see you…see you…

How could she expect him *not* to blame Cal?

A stinging sensation in his palms made him realize he was standing in the middle of the barn, clutching the wheelbarrow handles so tightly he was in danger of splitting the skin. With vicious force, he slammed open the door of the next stall and started shoveling the soiled straw.

As he put his back into the work, a pair of striking gray eyes floated across his mind, and he seized the opportunity to distract himself. With deliberate attention to detail he called up his memories of the pretty woman with whom he'd collided: full breasts; that too-wide, sexy mouth that had made him want to taste-test it; long, slender legs that were poured into her city girl jeans just right.... What in hell was a fine thing like that doing with Cal McCall?

Three hours later the morning chores were done. Marty's daughter, Cheyenne, was running a fever, and Marty couldn't go to the feed store as he'd planned, so Deck climbed into the truck and took off for town. He would swing by the feed store and then pick up the antibiotic the doctor had called in for Cheyenne.

It was a blindingly sunny spring day, and the alfalfa already was tall enough to ripple in a mild breeze. He jammed his hat firmly on his head and drove with the windows down, fingers drumming on the wheel in tempo with Garth Brooks on the radio.

There were a few other trucks in the feed store parking lot when he pulled in. As he slammed the door of the Ford and took the two steps to the front porch of the store in one stride, Stumpie Mohler nodded from his seat in the single rocking chair set amid the barrels and sacks.

"Morning, Stumpie."

"Morning, Deck. What can we do for you today?"

Deck just looked at him. What the heck did Stumpie think he needed...ice cream? "Feed."

Stumpie cackled. He'd been a cowhand until three years ago when he'd gotten an arm smashed by a bull and had to have it amputated. Sev Andressen, who owned the feed store, had employed him since then, although it was a standing joke in the community that Sev was paying Stumpie to keep the seat of that rocking chair warm.

"Ain't gonna get hot enough to work up a good sweat," the little man proclaimed. Then he cleared his throat ostentatiously. "You heard the news?"

Deck considered. "On the way in here, I heard there's

no rain in sight. And I heard the school board's considering a tax increase and there's a new crisis in the Middle East.''

Stumpie hawked and spat into a cup he'd set nearby. ''Naw, that ain't nothing compared to *my* news.''

He wasn't going to get out of here without hearing what Stumpie had to say. Deck shook his head, and planted his butt on one of the barrels that lined the rail. ''Okay, let's hear it.''

Stumpie paused and his face registered consternation. ''Aw, heck, you ain't going to be happy when you hear this. It's a good thing you're sitting down.''

Deck crossed his arms and waited.

''Word has it you saw Cal McCall in town yesterday.''

Deck nodded. Life in a small town was a pain in the ass sometimes. '''Word' has it right. So?''

''He's bought back his daddy's place.''

It was a struggle not to show the shock that ripped through his composure. Deck dropped his gaze to the weathered gray boards of the flooring beneath him. *One…two…* He counted ten nails before he could trust himself to speak. ''Is that all?''

''Nope.'' Stumpie shook his head, eyeing Deck with wary fascination. ''He was in here this morning, asking about ordering feed. Told Sev he done quit his New York job and he's coming back for good.''

Deck registered the facts. McCall had worked in New York. His lip curled. A city boy. Figured. And he was planning to live here. ''Thanks for the news flash,'' he said. Rising from the barrel, he headed for the door of the store to give Sev his order.

Not for anything would he let anyone see how the news had shaken him. McCall back here for good? And living on the ranch where he'd grown up? His boots hammered the floor with unnecessary force as he approached the counter where Sev was doing something on a little computer he'd recently installed.

"Morning, Deck." The big, burly man took one good look at him and added, "I see Stumpie's already broadcast the news."

"Yep." Deck fished in his pocket for the list he'd made. The mares needed some special oats, and Marty had added a few other things as well.

Sev took the piece of paper. "Guess it brings back some sad memories for you."

"I can think of ones I'd like better." Deck gestured to the list. "You got everything?"

"Yeah. I'll help you load it." He strode around the counter to the front door. "Stump, get in here and cover the phone while I load Deck."

"You betcha," came the reply. The little man hustled in the door as Sev led the way out.

With Sev's help the loading took no time. Ten minutes later Deck was bumping across the gravel street that led to the drugstore.

But when he approached the counter, the pharmacist shook his head apologetically. "It'll be a few more minutes, Deck. Sorry. It's been one of those mornings."

So he cooled his heels wandering around the drugstore while he waited for the prescription. He was standing in front of the magazine rack when someone else came around the nearest corner and he glanced up automatically.

It was *Silver Eyes*! The woman from the grocery store. Cal McCall's woman. She stopped dead when she saw him blocking her path.

Today she was wearing black jeans with a white sleeveless shirt that dipped low in the front, showing smooth tanned skin that swelled gently as it disappeared behind the barrier of the fabric. Her eyes were as luminous and bright as they'd been the previous evening as she returned his gaze. Then one corner of her mouth quirked.

"We really must stop meeting in the aisles like this." Her smile widened, and her eyes warmed with amusement. She put out a hand. "I'm Silver Jenssen."

Deck looked down at the slim hand she extended. What would her bare skin feel like? Would she be as soft and silky as she looked? He realized she was still standing before him with her hand out, so he slowly put out his own hand and grasped hers.

Her skin was as soft as he'd imagined. No, softer. Her hand was much smaller than his and her skin was smooth as silky fabric. He brushed his thumb back and forth across her knuckles. She was staring at him but those pretty eyes looked puzzled and her smile began to fade. He realized he was staring at her again, just like yesterday. And she was waiting for an answer to her friendly gesture.

"Deck Stryker." He cocked his head to one side. "Silver for the eyes?"

She nodded. "My mother has them, too. I was going to be named Paula after my father, Paul, but Mama said she knew the minute I opened my eyes that I was Silver." She grimaced. "Thank heavens. I can't imagine being named Paula."

Silver suited her better. He still held her hand. "You're new in town."

Her expression altered again, warming. He'd have to try harder to act like a normal human being. Then again, she belonged to McCall so why did it matter what she thought of him?

"Yes, I am," she said. "I'm just visiting, though, for a month or two."

"You have family here?" If she'd ever been to Kadoka before, he was positive he'd remember her. And he was dying to know how she'd gotten hooked up with McCall.

She tugged discreetly at her hand, and he let her go reluctantly. "My brother used to live here," she said. "He just moved back to town."

"Your brother?" He felt like somebody had hit him right over the head with a two-by-four. Kadoka was a tiny little town. It wasn't possible that *two* of its own were returning to live at the exact same time. Which meant…she was Cal's sister. She was a *McCall?* But she'd said her name was Jenssen. His mind raced. He'd grown up with Cal and he'd never seen hide nor hair of a sister.

But it was coming back to him now.

No, he'd never seen her, but he knew Cal had a sister. His mama had left his daddy when Cal was still a baby and gone back East to her family. Cal and his daddy stayed on the prairie, and the mother had married some fancy Virginian. This mouthwatering morsel must be the half sister Cal had mentioned from time to time.

She was speaking, and he forced himself to attend to what she was saying.

"…probably know my brother. Cal McCall? I came for a few weeks to help him get the house cleaned up and organized." She paused. "Is Deck short for something? It's an unusual name."

"Deckett," he told her. "My middle name, my mother's before she married."

"Your first name's that bad?" Her eyes twinkled.

He nodded. "George. I'm not a George."

"No," she agreed, looking him over as if comparing him with the name. "You're not a George."

"Hey, Deck!" The pharmacist's bellow was guaranteed

to be heard all over the store. "Your prescription's ready."

"That's my signal to get moving." He hesitated, knowing that once she told her brother who she'd met she very likely wouldn't even speak to him next time their paths crossed. "You enjoy your visit to South Dakota."

"Thank you. I'll be here for several more weeks, so I'm sure I'll see you again."

There was nothing he could say to that, so he didn't even try. Nodding once, he turned and went off to pick up the medicine Marty had sent him for.

"I'll be fine. Stop worrying!" Silver hunched her shoulder high to hold the cordless phone to her ear as she carried a stack of dishes from a packing crate to the newly cleaned and papered shelf she was filling.

"I know." She could hear the rueful humor in Cal's voice. "Old habits die hard. You've been my baby sister for a long time."

"Well, your baby sister's twenty-six years old now and perfectly capable of staying alone on a ranch for two weeks. I'll be so busy organizing this house the time will fly."

"I really am sorry," Cal said, for what seemed like the tenth time. "I had all the loose ends tied up in New York. But I owed this guy a big favor, and when he called I couldn't say no."

She was tired of listening to her brother apologize. "I'm almost done with the kitchen," she said. "Do you have a preference for how I go about this or shall I just dig in?"

"Whatever." Cal obviously hadn't been kidding when he'd told her she could do whatever she wanted to the house once the carpenters were done. "I have to go. Thanks again, little sis. I owe you one."

"No problem. This is a vacation for me, honestly. Take care of yourself. I'll see you in two weeks."

They said their goodbyes, and Silver set down another load of dishes to punch the off button on the phone. As she replaced the phone in the cradle, she realized she'd forgotten to ask Cal if he remembered Deck Stryker from his growing-up days.

Deck.

Golden-brown hair, worn too long under the black hat she had yet to see him without. Too-serious eyes the same dark-blue as the sky right before a summer storm. A mouth with confident, chiseled lips that should smile more often. Come to think of it, she'd never seen him smile at all. She had a feeling that if Deck Stryker ever smiled at her, she'd humiliate herself by kissing the ground at his feet. He was the sexiest man she'd ever met.

That first time, when she'd smacked into him in the grocery aisle, she'd have sworn she'd been struck by lightning when his hands had reached out to steady her. Just for a moment, before he'd set her away, she'd felt the lean, hard contours of his body and had found it hard to draw a steady breath.

The second time, in the drugstore yesterday, she shouldn't have been quite so *overwhelmed* by the man. But when he'd taken the hand she extended, she'd gotten the same jittery feeling she'd had the day before, as if she couldn't get a deep-enough breath after running a five-minute mile. And then he'd just held her hand...and held it and held it until finally she'd gently reclaimed it as her own. He hadn't smiled once the whole time, either, but those intense blue eyes had devoured every inch of her until he had her more flustered than she'd been when she'd knocked into him the day before that.

If she were looking for a man, she'd definitely look twice at Deck. But the last thing she needed, the *very last,* was more man trouble. It would be a cold day in hell before she got suckered by sweet words and promises again.

She picked up a china plate from the stack she'd just unwrapped and slid it into the soapy water in which she was washing all the kitchenware before arranging it in Cal's cupboards and the pretty china closet in the dining room. No, she was too smart to get involved with another man.

Rinsing the soapy dish, her attention was caught by the sparkle of the golden trim on the delicate, fluted edge of the plate. She'd been given a ring that color once. She shuddered to think how close she'd come to marrying the toad who had given it to her, too. Chet had seemed different from the others who'd been more impressed by her family's bank account than by her as a person. But just like the others, he'd wanted a shortcut to Easy Street, and she'd almost given it to him before she'd seen the truth.

Her morose reflections were interrupted by a knock on the door. Now, who could that be? It wasn't as if people stopped in off the main road for a chat when the ranch house was two miles back from the highway. Briskly she wiped her hands on a dish towel, slinging it over her shoulder as she walked through the mudroom to the back door and pulled it open.

On the other side stood a girl. Or maybe a woman. She was so skinny it was hard to tell.

Both the girl's eyes were mottled with old yellow-and-green bruising and there was an ugly red welt along her jaw. A cut snaked up to mar her lower lip line on the left side, and Silver caught her breath at the sight of raw flesh where the mark had split the skin...skin that was dirty and dulled with dust and Heaven only knew what else. On her forehead was a lump the size of a tennis ball, which was red and purpling even as she watched. Silver knew she'd been sheltered from some of life's harsher realities, but this wasn't a sight she expected to find on Cal's back porch first thing in the morning.

"Hello," said the girl in a hoarse whisper. "M-may I use your telephone?"

"Of course." Silver opened the door wide and reached out to draw her unexpected guest inside.

The girl jerked away from her outstretched hand in a reflex so automatic Silver knew without any previous experience that she'd expected to be hit.

Raising both hands in the air to show she was harmless, Silver stepped back from the door. Her heart twisted with pity. "It's all right," she said, pitching her voice low and soothing. "Come on in and I'll show you where the phone is."

The girl's eyelids fluttered as she measured Silver. She nodded. "Thank you, ma'am," she whispered. She stepped over the threshold, paused, threw a puzzled, almost imploring glance at her hostess—

And before Silver realized what was happening, her guest's eyes rolled up in her head and her knees buckled. Silver sprang forward with a startled exclamation, barely catching the girl's head before it hit the floor. Gently she eased the poor thing into a supine position, grabbing the dish towel off her shoulder and folding it to put beneath the girl's head. It was a bit damp but that was the least of her problems right now.

Rising, she rushed across the room and grabbed the telephone. She stared at it for a second, then dropped it back into place. *Forget it, Silver! The hospital's too far away.* An ambulance would take forever to arrive. Cal had warned her before he left about the lack of convenient medical care. This girl needed immediate help.

There was an emergency clinic in Kadoka. She knew because Cal had mentioned it in his "this is different from what you're used to" speech. She knelt beside the girl again and felt for a pulse. Silver didn't know much about first aid but she thought the steady beat beneath her seeking fingers felt pretty strong so she rose and rushed out the door, grabbing the keys to Cal's brand-new three-quarter-ton pickup. She pulled the vehicle around to the side of the porch and opened the back door, then ran into the house and checked the girl again.

She was still unconscious. Her body was slender to the point of being gaunt beneath the filthy jeans and torn T-shirt but Silver doubted she could lift her. Before she'd fallen, the girl had been every bit as tall as Silver herself.

Walking around behind the girl's head, she eased her hands beneath her skull and lifted it into an upright position against her legs. Then she got her hands beneath the girl's armpits and straightened. The head lolled alarmingly but there was no help for it so she threw her energy into pulling the girl across the floor and out the door onto the porch, down off the stoop to the side of the truck.

She paused for a moment, trying to decide how best to get the woman's limp body into the pickup. A drop of sweat trickled down the side of her face, and she ducked her head and wiped it on her shoulder before pulling the girl forward again. Scrambling backward, she strained to lift the girl far enough to get her body up on the seat.

She kept going until the far door stopped her progress. Reaching behind her, she opened it and backed out, laying the girl out across the front seat. After she checked to be sure the girl's head wasn't going to get bumped when she closed the door she slammed it shut and dashed around the hood to the driver's side.

Gunning the engine, she began the drive out the lane as fast as she dared, worrying that she would jar the girl off the seat onto the floor if she was too rough. As soon as she got on the paved road, she could make better time. It occurred to her that there might be someone around who could help if only she could get their attention, so she laid on the horn as she drove, blaring a raucous signal into the still air until the sound made her head hurt.

When she crested the last little hill before the road, relief rose within her. But then relief turned to incredulous concern when she saw the battered blue pickup truck sideways across the lane, its hood crumpled into one of the stone pillars that marked the entrance to the ranch. Good Lord! Had the girl walked all the way back the lane from here? It seemed impossible. Hastily she braked to a halt, praying that the girl was all right as she jumped out and ran to inspect the damaged truck.

The front of the truck was a dented mess of metal. On the driver's side the door hung open and a seat belt hung half out the door. That explained why the driver hadn't been thrown through the windshield. Quickly she circled the truck. It occurred to her that perhaps the girl hadn't been alone, and her mouth went dry at the prospect of yet another injured person.

But no one else appeared to have been with the girl. Silver glanced back at her vehicle, measuring the space between the bed of the truck and the farther stone column. There was no way she could get through there. And she couldn't go around because the fence ran right up to the entrance.

But she *had* to get this girl to a doctor! Who knew

what could be wrong with her? She hurried back to her own truck and scrambled in, reaching for the phone Cal had had installed in all the ranch vehicles. Looked like she'd have to call for help anyway.

That's when she heard the sound of another truck coming down the road.

Dropping the phone, she got out again and ran to the edge of the road. The sun was in her eyes and she shielded them with one hand as she waved the other in a frantic beckoning. *Please stop! Oh, please, please stop.*

A black pickup slowed, and its tires crunched in the gravel, raising billowing ribbons of dust as it braked and the driver's door opened. Silver moved forward.

"Could you help me, please? I found—Deck!" She was taken aback when the man who'd been in her dreams all morning climbed from his truck.

By the time she recovered, he was already moving past her. "I heard your horn. Anybody hurt?"

"Y-yes. In my truck. She knocked on my door this morning." She trotted behind him as he strode past the wreck of the blue pickup to her own vehicle. "She fainted. I was taking her to the hospital but I couldn't get by."

"I'll drive. Get your stuff." He yanked open the passenger door and leaned in, easily hefting the woman in his arms. While Silver was still staring at him stupidly, he turned and strode toward his truck.

"My stuff?" she echoed stupidly.

He turned and gave her an impatient look. "Aren't you coming along?"

Her gaze flicked to her own truck and back again. "I—"

"I need you to hold her. I'll bring you home again later."

"Oh. All right." She flew to her truck and grabbed the purse she'd flung onto the floor, then locked the doors before pocketing the keys and hurrying around to the passenger door of Deck's truck.

It was higher than hers and she had to scramble a bit to get in. The minute she had her seat belt on, he lifted the woman across Silver, placing her in the center seat. Silver caught her weight as she slumped sideways, and eased the woman's head into the crook of her arm. As Silver supported her weight, Deck slipped his arms from beneath his burden. His face was so near that his lips would brush over hers if she turned her head. As he withdrew from the truck, his arm slid across Silver's stomach, perilously close to the underside of her breasts.

She nearly jumped out of her seat at the contact, brief as it was. If he noticed, he didn't show any sign.

Deck came around and slid behind the wheel, turning onto the road again with smooth, economical movements and moving along at a fast clip toward town. He picked up a cell phone and punched some buttons, then waited for a moment and began to speak.

"Sev? Deck. I'm bringing Lyn Hamill in. She's unconscious, looks like she wrecked her truck."

He waited while the person on the other end spoke, then replied, "Hold on." He turned to Silver. "How long's she been out?"

Silver shrugged. "Probably close to thirty minutes."

"Thirty minutes," Deck reported. "But she was conscious right afterward. She got back to the McCall place somehow. McCall's sister answered the door, and Lyn collapsed."

He listened again. "No blood that I can see, anyway." He glanced at Silver with a question in his eyes and she shook her head. "We'll be there in twenty."

Abruptly Deck shut off the phone. There was a silence in the truck. Silver's mind was whirling. "How did you hear my horn?"

"I'm your neighbor. Next place over." He didn't sound very pleased about it.

She leaned her head against the back of the seat and closed her eyes for a moment. "I appreciate your help. I guess I'll have to call a tow truck to move that truck from the entrance to the lane."

"Your brother can do it with your truck." His voice sounded almost challenging, and she wondered if he was annoyed with her or the situation.

"My brother's out of town for a couple of weeks," she said. She hesitated. "Deck, I'm sorry for inconveniencing you. I could have called an emergency team."

"Around here folks help each other," he said. "I was going to town, anyway." He glanced at the girl in her arms, still ominously quiet, and she saw his eyes soften. "Besides, Lynnie's had enough trouble in her life. Folks'll appreciate you helping her."

"Who is she?" She didn't like the way his obvious affection for the girl made her feel. How could she possibly be jealous with a man she barely knew?

"Local girl. Her father owned the McCall outfit for a while. She's had it tough."

"How old is she?"

Deck shrugged. "Couple years younger than me?" He measured her. "I'm twenty-seven. I'd say Lyn's closer to your age. You're...about twenty-five now?"

"Twenty-six." Then his words penetrated. "You must have grown up with my brother."

"He and my brother are the same age." Deck's voice was flat, and she thought she must be annoying him with her chatter.

Turning her head, she looked out the window. They were rolling through mile after mile of prairie. When Cal had driven her out here the first time, she'd been amazed at the isolation. It had seemed as if a person could drive for days without seeing another house. Of course, she'd come to realize that was an exaggeration. Hours maybe, but not days.

The still form in her arms stirred and groaned, and instantly Silver was alert. "It's all right, Lyn," she murmured. "You're safe."

"Wha…?" The girl's hands fluttered. Then, before Silver could offer her any additional reassurance she slipped back into the limp, unresponsive posture.

Silver lifted her gaze to see Deck glancing at them both in clear concern. "I don't know anything about brain injury," she said, "but this is scaring me."

"We'll be there soon." To her astonishment Deck reached across the seat and laid a hand across hers where she clasped Lyn Hamill's elbow. He squeezed gently, a firm, warm pressure that made her long to turn her own palm up and slide her fingers through his. "You did a good thing."

Two

―――

She was pacing.

Deck watched as Silver sprang to her feet yet again and walked to the corner of the waiting area at the clinic. What the hell was he doing waiting here with her? It had been damn bad luck that he'd been the first one to come across her this morning.

He'd heard that horn and recognized it as some kind of trouble. He'd been stopped by the pasture dam, checking the water level in the dam, and it hadn't taken him any time at all to investigate. When he realized who it was at the entrance to the McCall place, he'd had an impulse to drive on past just to save himself the aggravation. She was McCall's sister. He ought to be staying as far away from her as possible.

Then he'd seen Lynnie Hamill and realized he couldn't drive away and leave either woman.

But that didn't explain why he was hanging around the

clinic. He shouldn't want to be anywhere near here. Near *her*.

He watched as she walked the perimeter of the room again. She peered around the corner for a long moment before turning and walked a slow circuit around the room, finally coming to a stop before the single window.

She clearly hadn't been planning on going anywhere this morning. She wore a pair of skin-tight old jeans that were white at the stress points, tennis sneakers that probably had been white once and an oversize T-shirt. The fabric was pulled into a knot at the waist, draping softly over her breasts in a manner that left his mouth dry and his body reminding him that he'd been without a woman too long. Her dark hair was as wildly curly as it had been the first day he'd seen her, though she had nothing in it today. It flew around her shoulders from a side part with each new motion.

Motion. Ah, the woman definitely could move. He couldn't remember ever seeing a filly with such pretty action before in his whole entire life. Though he wasn't fond of fidgety women he enjoyed the contained energy in her stride, the flex of supple muscle beneath her jeans, the slender rhythm of her hips.

He could think of ways he'd enjoy those hips even more. His body reacted as it had every time he'd so much as thought of Silver Jenssen in the past few days, and he shifted uncomfortably on the thin pad of the waiting room chair. He was starting to feel like his stallion penned next to a mare in season. Every time he'd looked at the poor critter, the horse had been more than ready to do his manly duty. A man couldn't help but feel sympathy for such frustration.

He rose, unable to resist getting just a little closer and

walked over to her. "You might as well stop fretting," he advised her. "Sev said the ambulance'll be here soon."

"I know." Silver didn't turn from the window. "I'm just so afraid for her…"

He lifted his hands. After a second's hesitation he clasped her shoulders in his palms, rubbing gently at the knots of tension he felt there. The feel of her softness beneath his hands made his fingers clench in automatic reaction before he got the surge of lust under control. "She was married to a first-class bastard," he said. "They were divorced but I heard he wouldn't stop coming around."

Silver's whole body had stilled beneath his touch. She rolled her shoulders and tilted her head to one side, giving him unspoken permission to continue his massage. "I don't think all those marks on her face were from the accident," she said. "Some of them weren't fresh." She turned and looked up at him, and her mouth was firm. "I won't let her be abused anymore," she said.

Deck knew he should take his hands from her shoulders now that she was facing him. It was too much like an embrace, and the last person in the world he ought to be hugging was Cal McCall's sister.

But her flesh was warm and soft beneath his hands, and her eyes were so troubled that he couldn't just walk off. "I haven't seen her in a long time," he said. "Nobody has."

"If she needs a place, she can stay with me," Silver said.

"Your brother might not be too thrilled with that." He didn't know why he'd felt compelled to bring Cal into the conversation, but the mention of his name banished the aura of intimacy.

"Cal wouldn't mind," she said confidently, though he

thought he saw a flicker of doubt in her eyes for a moment. "Besides, he needs me to get his house in order, so he owes me one." Then her face fell and she sighed heavily. "I hate sending her off to a strange hospital all alone. Maybe I should go along."

He shuddered. He couldn't prevent it, couldn't conceal the revulsion that he knew showed on his face. It was all he could do to tolerate a place like this. Hospitals...he hadn't been able to force himself to set foot in one since the terrible hours after Genie's accident. The smell made him nauseous, the hushed atmosphere made him want to jump up and shout, the sight of people in white coats rushing around flat out scared the hell out of him.

"There's no call for that," he said aloud. "She'll be in good hands."

"It's not that." She looked up at him earnestly. "I just don't want her to wake up alone without a friend. That girl looked like she could use a friend."

With her face tipped up, those wide eyes so serious, she was all but irresistible. His gaze slid down to her mouth, noting the parted lips, the nervous habit she had of nibbling on the bottom one when something was upsetting her as it had been today.

She was Cal McCall's sister, he told himself. He shouldn't be talking to her, much less touching her.

Why not? whispered a little voice inside. *He took your sister. It would be the perfect revenge.*

Right. Like getting cozy with Silver Jenssen could make up for what he'd lost. No one in the world would ever understand. Part of himself had died, too, when Genie had died. A part that could never be regained or replaced.

"Deck?"

He focused on the present again, and there she stood,

those beautiful eyes with their dark-rimmed irises looking at him with concern. What the hell—he had to have just one little taste.

"Are you all right?" She spoke again.

He cleared his throat. "I'm fine. Except that I'm holding the prettiest woman in town in my arms and I haven't kissed her yet."

Surprise flared in her eyes. Then, before he could lower his head, she stepped backward out from under his hands. "I wish that ambulance would get here."

The minute she finished the sentence a door banged down the hall and heavy footsteps moved rapidly in their direction. Deck stepped away from Silver and looked out the window.

He hadn't expected her to rebuff his advance. True, she barely knew him, but he could say without false modesty that he'd kissed a whole lot of women who'd spent even less time with him. He didn't often make the effort to pursue, because he didn't need to. He guessed that in this case he might have to make that effort. The primitive hunter within him stirred and woke. Oh, yes, he'd definitely have to make the effort.

Sev Andressen came into the room, a white hospital-style coat over his jeans and shirt. "She's still unconscious," he reported. "The ambulance is coming in right now."

"I'm going along with her," Silver said. "I won't be able to give them much, but I'll explain it."

"Wait a minute," said Deck. "You can't do that."

Silver raised one eyebrow as she turned to look at him. "Why not?"

"Because...because..." He was floundering and he knew it. "You don't have transportation."

"She can ride along," said Sev. Then he turned as the

scream of the approaching ambulance became audible. "We'd better get ready. These guys don't fool around."

The next few minutes were a blur of activity. The medical technicians rushed in with a gurney, and the patient was transferred to it. Then Deck and Sev helped the two men carry the gurney back to the ambulance and load it. Silver followed them and when the cot was safely installed, the technicians scrambled in and one extended a hand to her.

Silver stepped forward, but before she could climb in, Deck stopped her with a hand on her arm. "I'll come to the hospital tonight."

"You don't have to do that."

"You need a way home," he told her. Was he crazy to be pushing this?

She tossed him an impatient glance. "I can rent a car."

He shook his head, ducking it as a gust of spring wind threatened to unseat his hat. "I'll be there tonight."

"Ready?" The driver turned and gestured at Silver to hurry. "Let's get moving."

Without giving Deck another glance, Silver pulled herself into the ambulance and the technician slammed the doors. But as the vehicle began to pick up speed, Silver turned to the window. She met his gaze, unsmiling, but she wiggled her fingers at him in farewell.

As hospital furniture went, this wasn't so bad.

Silver pulled up the footrest on the reclining lounger and propped her feet on its cushion, idly flipping the channels on the wall-mounted television with the remote. In the bed beside her chair Lyn Hamill, her unexpected guest from early this morning, lay quietly. She had yet to move or speak.

It was ten minutes before eight in the evening, and visiting hours would be over shortly. Maybe Deck had had second thoughts about his promise after he thought about the way she'd rejected his flirtation at the clinic.

He'd looked so disappointed when she'd backed away from him. She knew just how he'd felt. A part of her longed to lift herself on tiptoe and press her mouth to his, to trace the stern line of his lips and touch her tongue to the small cleft that divided his squared-off chin. A shiver worked its way down her spine at the notion, coming to rest deep in her abdomen where it throbbed restlessly. She shifted in the chair.

Stop it, girl. You came out here to get away from man trouble, not find it! Amen to that, she thought, giving in to a huge yawn.

And then "man trouble" walked through the door. Hastily she stifled the yawn and lowered the footrest on the chair as Deck hesitated in the entrance.

"Hello," she said. "I was beginning to think you took me seriously."

His face seemed pale beneath the artificial light and he was sweating slightly. As he removed his hat, he swiped a hand across his forehead before resettling the hat in its place. "I told you I'd take you home," he reminded her.

She didn't know what to say to that, so she focused instead on the huge vase of fresh wildflowers he carried in one big hand. "Those are beautiful. What a thoughtful idea." He extended the vase and she took it from him, turning to carry it to the single windowsill. "This room needed something to brighten it up."

"Looks like you beat me to that." He glanced around at the helium-filled balloons she had tied in two bunches, one to the wardrobe door handle and the other to the foot rail of the sturdy hospital bed.

She shrugged as she dipped a finger in the vase to check

the water level. "I figured it might help if she woke up to something cheerful."

He nodded, then swiped his hand down the side of his face. "Are you ready to go now?"

"I suppose." She hesitated. "I thought about staying overnight in case she woke up, but the doctors don't have any idea how long this state might last. Could be hours, could be days." Could be forever. "And I have animals to feed."

"Your brother has stock already?" Deck sounded surprised. "And no help?"

"We don't need help yet," she said. "All that's on the ranch right now are two dogs, a mother cat and kittens and one cantankerous she-goat left by the previous owner."

She moved around the room, straightening the chair and lying the television remote and a pitcher of water beside a full glass on the rolling tray which she parked within reach at the bedside should Lyn awake. She checked to be sure the nurses' call button was within plain sight and finally took her purse from the wardrobe, empty except for the tattered remnants of clothing the girl had been wearing. She had a list of Lyn's clothing sizes in her purse now. "I'm ready."

She took Lyn's hand again one more time before letting Deck escort her from the room. "I'm going home for the night," she told the unresponsive girl, "but I'll come back. You just rest and get well."

Deck didn't speak as they took the elevator down and traipsed through the corridors to the main entrance where he'd parked. In the parking lot she recognized his truck immediately.

One thing she could say, she thought as he opened her door and offered her a hand, the man had good manners.

She was feminine enough to enjoy and be grateful for the small courtesies that a former generation would have taken for granted.

"Have you eaten?" It was the first thing he said as he drove away from the medical building.

"Um, I had some crackers earlier, and I ate a little of the lunch they brought to Lyn's room." She made a face. "I'd forgotten how bad hospital food is."

He glanced across at her. "You've been hospitalized before?"

"No." She shook her head and laughed. "I'm healthy as a horse. My mother had some minor surgery last year, so I had the chance to enjoy hospital cuisine then."

He nodded. End of conversation.

Silver surveyed his profile as he drove through the city. The man talked less than anyone she'd ever met. Did he do it on purpose or was he just that reticent? She'd told him numerous little snippets of information in the few times they'd met, and she still knew next to nothing about him. Well. That was about to change.

"So tell me about yourself," she said.

Silence. Finally he looked across at her and she caught the first glint of humor in his eye that she'd seen since she met him. "You first."

"Okay." If that would get him talking, she'd be glad to start. "You know I have a half brother. I was born in Virginia, raised near Charlottesville as an only child until Cal came to live with us when I was twelve. I studied for four years to get a teaching degree I've never used. Cal invited me out here when he bought his father's place. I'm spending a month or two helping him get the house in order."

"And then what?"

"Pardon?"

"Will you go home again?"

She shook her head, smiling. "How did you know that's the one thing I can't answer?"

He arched an eyebrow, his gaze still on the street, but he didn't say anything.

She didn't say anything, either, for a moment. But eventually she couldn't stand the silence. "I don't really want to go home. I've been thinking of visiting a friend in London."

"Why don't you want to go home?"

She shrugged. "I feel sort of in the way if you want the truth. Mother and Daddy are retired, ready to travel and enjoy life, but I think they feel that if I'm around they still need to be there. Plus they're determined to marry me off."

He glanced at her, one long arm draped over the steering wheel with utter assurance. "Anyone in particular?"

She laughed but she didn't really think the question was funny. "Oh, they're particular, all right. Particularly determined to find me the perfect Southern gentleman. Yuck." She crossed her arms. "That's the big reason I don't want to go home."

"So get a job and get your own place."

She wasn't about to tell him that she could afford several of her own places without ever lifting a finger. "That's sound advice." She paused. "Your turn."

"My turn to what?"

"Talk." She shook a finger playfully at him. "I just told you my life story. Now it's your turn."

He lifted a shoulder as he flipped on the turn signal. "My brother Marty and I inherited the family ranch when my dad passed away nine years ago. Six years ago, my mother married a widower from Sioux Falls and they moved to Florida. She's still there enjoying the sunshine."

He braked and shifted the truck into park, gesturing out the window with his hand. "Let's get something to eat."

She hadn't been paying attention and she was startled to see that they were parked in the lot of a bar and grill kind of restaurant. She glanced down at the ratty old clothing she'd been wearing since the early-morning hours. "I hope they don't dress up in there."

"Smile at them," Deck advised as he came around and opened her door. "They'll never know what you're wearing."

In the act of sliding down from the seat of the truck she paused, looking up at him with surprise. "Thank you," she said. "That was a lovely compliment."

Deck's lips twitched. She wondered what it would take to get him to smile. "Enjoy it. I'm not much on flowery talk."

"I'm not one who needs it," she told him.

To her shock, he lifted a hand and smoothed a quirky tendril of hair back from her cheek, his rough fingers brushing over her sensitive skin. "Maybe not, but you deserve it."

She opened her mouth, realized she had no earthly idea how to respond to that and closed it again.

Deck stepped away and took her elbow as she slipped down from the high seat, then slammed the door and started toward the restaurant, still cupping her elbow. A low sound caught her ear, and she glanced at him, surprised and startled. "Are you laughing?"

He shrugged, his expression a perfect poker face. "It's good to know that paying you a compliment shuts you up."

They ate sitting at the bar in the big room in the front of the restaurant, and she was grateful to Deck. The other patrons looked as if they'd come straight from their barns and her faded clothing wasn't a problem at all. There were several cowboys there who knew Deck, and if she was the only one who noticed he barely had to utter a word in all the chattering the other men did, nobody said anything. Then again, if he was always like this, they'd be used to it, wouldn't they?

While she drank a cup of coffee to help ward off the exhaustion that was rolling over her, Deck slid off his stool beside her and walked a few feet away to talk to a couple of men seated in one of the booths.

A jean-clad thigh pressing against hers jolted her out of her stupor. Startled, she slid her leg away, but the man who'd plopped himself down on the next stool only spread himself out more until his thigh pressed against hers again, leaning one elbow on the bar and smiling at her.

He was young and cocky—that was the first thing she noticed. Definitely a bad case of the "what-a-prize-I-am" syndrome.

The second thing she noticed was his hand. It hovered over her thigh for a moment, then settled just above her knee as if it belonged there. Without thinking, she reached down and picked it up, deliberately placing it on the bar. "Excuse me, but I'm not part of the furniture."

"I didn't think you were, sweet thing." He leaned closer, smiling at her with big blue eyes that probably got him results most of the time. "I'm Jeffery. Can I buy you a drink while we get to know each other?"

"No, thank you." She turned back to her coffee, hoping he'd take the hint, but of course someone so sure of his own charm couldn't believe she wasn't interested.

"Okay. How bout we go dancing? You look like a girl who's got rhythm."

She was tempted to tell him his pickup lines needed serious work. Instead, she kept looking into her coffee.

"Aw, come on, gorgeous, I can tell you and I have a lot in common. My truck's right outside—"

"And if you want to live to drive it again you'd better get your ass back in it now." The voice came from behind them, low and flat and deadly serious.

Jeffery turned around belligerently, but when he saw the tall, dark-featured cowboy in the black hat, he held up both hands in a placatory gesture. "Sorry, buddy. She was sitting here all alone. I didn't know she was taken."

"Get out." Deck's voice cracked like a whip.

The younger man's eyes flared wide, and he scrambled off the stool so fast he nearly fell. As he beat a hasty retreat, Deck's eyes met Silver's. The deep black anger in them shocked her. "Are you about finished there?"

She nodded. Her legs were trembling, but she stood obediently and let him lead her out of the bar. There was an aura of leashed violence that surrounded Deck in an almost tangible manner. Still, she was a modern woman.

"I could have handled him, but thank you for your assistance. Your method undoubtedly worked faster than mine would have."

They walked across the gravel to his truck as she spoke. Leading her around to the passenger side, he opened the door and she slid in quickly, avoiding his eyes. He still didn't speak. What was he thinking? He was definitely annoyed—he wasn't angry with *her,* was he?

"What's the matter with you?" she demanded as he paced back to the driver's side and slid in. "You're acting like I did something wrong."

He shook his head and slid the key into the ignition, then fired up the engine.

"Wait a minute." She grabbed his arm before he put the truck in gear. "Don't you ignore me!"

The words had barely left her mouth before he reached for her, taking her upper arms and hauling her over the seat into his lap. Tipping her backward so that she had to clutch at his shoulders for balance, he looked down into her startled face. "I don't like seeing another man's hands on you." His voice was deep and harsh, his features fierce.

The words would never qualify as romantic, but his rough, matter-of-fact statement touched a waiting heat deep in her body. Her heart seemed to drop to the pit of her stomach and she inhaled a sharp breath, her heartbeat speeding up until it hammered in her throat like a trapped bird at a window.

And as she stared at him, stunned and needy, he lowered his head and took her mouth.

His lips were firm, warm and not in the least tentative. With bold intent, he molded her mouth until she whimpered deep in her throat. The world receded and all she could feel was the hot demand of his mouth, the strength in his corded arms as his hands came around her to pull her hard against him.

"Kiss me," he growled against the sealed line of her lips. His arms felt like two steel bands holding her in place, and his body was so hot she could feel him burning her right through her clothing. *"Kiss me."*

She'd never been manhandled like this in her life.

She loved it.

Like soft butter she melted against him, opening her mouth to admit his tongue, and it was as if her small yielding ripped away whatever restraints Deck had placed on himself. His tongue plunged into her mouth and plunged again. He pulled her more fully across his lap,

lying across his lap as she was, his arms turning her and
drawing her even closer until her breasts were flattened
against his hard chest. His right hand roved from her waist
down over the curve of her bottom to her thigh, and she
felt his palm curl around her, dragging her leg up so that
she was curled around him like a honeysuckle vine.

She slid her hands from his shoulders up and over his
back, exploring the hard, taut muscles that rippled beneath
his shirt. He'd obviously showered before coming to
town, and he smelled of soap and cologne, his scent teasing her senses as his tongue played over hers. She raised
one hand to his neck, sliding it up into his golden-brown
hair and then back down to the heated silky flesh of his
nape, stroking her fingers dreamily over his skin. How
could one man be so arousing?

He kissed her and kissed her until she was moaning in
his arms, her mouth following his when he lifted his head
to change the angle. His hat was in the way, and he swept
it off with an impatient hand. When he lowered his hand
again, he rested it on her rib cage right below her breasts.
Slowly but surely, he smoothed his palm upward over the
fabric of her T-shirt, over the aching mound of her breast,
filling his hand with her. He explored her like that for a
while, his thumb and index finger coaxing her nipple up
into a tight little bead that he rolled until electric lines of
sensation zinged straight from her nipple to her loins,
making her ache and shift her hips restlessly. Against her
hip, she could feel the hard ridge of his erection, and the
knowledge that she'd aroused him, too, was a heady pleasure that only excited her more.

But after another long moment of kissing and petting,
she sensed an easing in the frantic quality of his first
kisses.

Slowly, he withdrew his hand from her breast and slid

it down to rest on her hip. Slowly, the hard arm around her back loosened and her body no longer felt as if it had been glued to his. Slowly, his kisses grew smaller and smaller until he was barely brushing light caresses over her lips. And finally he lifted his head.

"Whoa." It was a heartfelt exclamation of wonder. It amused her that the first thing he did was reach for his hat and resettle it on his head.

Her head still lay against his shoulder, her face turned up to his, and she smiled. "Well said."

"That's been on my mind since the first minute I saw you." His voice was a low rumble.

"And has your curiosity been satisfied?" *Hers* hadn't. Her whole body was throbbing with need.

His chest heaved against her as he snorted in silent laughter. "Not by a long shot, baby. That little teaser only makes me wonder what *more* will be like."

How was she supposed to respond to that? Agreement would mean she accepted that there would be more between them. And though her body still throbbed and begged for his touch, she wasn't at all sure this was a smart thing to do.

Instead of responding, she said, "I wondered what you looked like without your hat." She reached up to touch the brim but he caught her wrist in midair, then brought his lips to the tender flesh, nibbling small kisses along her arm.

"That's off-limits." His eyes gleamed when he glanced up at her from where he lingered over her wrist. He'd accepted the change of subject with good grace.

"What?" Her brain wasn't working well, although other parts of her body seemed to be humming along just fine.

His breath huffed over her skin as he chuckled. "Didn't you know? Never touch a cowboy's hat."

"Never touch a cowboy's hat," she repeated, trying to keep her mind on the conversation. "That's silly."

"Maybe so, but there are fellas who take it real seriously." He heaved an enormous sigh, then gently lifted her off his lap. "We'd better get going. It's a good drive back to Kadoka."

He turned the key and put the truck in gear, but when she went to put on her seat belt he patted the middle seat beside him. "Here."

So she slid over next to him and put on the center belt.

He put his arm around her and drew her head to his shoulder. "Why don't you close your eyes. Your day started out crazy and just got worse, didn't it?"

She made a wry sound of agreement as they drove through the streets back to the interstate, which cut through the town, and before the lights of Rapid City had faded behind them, she felt her eyelids growing heavier....

She awoke when he started bumping back the rough lane to her brother's ranch. Instantly she remembered the day's events and she sat up straighter. "What happened to Lyn's truck?"

"My brother and I moved it to the side of the road after I took your brother's truck back to your place," Deck replied. "Tomorrow I'll tow it in and see what the garage can do with it."

His arm was still around her shoulders as they completed the drive, but she felt tense and awkward now. What had she been thinking, letting him kiss and touch her like that in a parking lot in plain sight of anybody who walked by? Her body tensed at the memory, and she knew exactly what she'd been thinking. And if they'd done that right there in that parking lot, they might have gotten arrested. Her face grew hot and she was glad when he slowed and braked before the house. She got out on her side before he could come around and he walked around the truck to accompany her to the door.

"Deck, I—" But she never finished the sentence.

He curled his hand around the back of her neck and his face loomed in her vision for a moment until she shut her eyes, then his lips covered hers. This time his lips were less demanding, the kiss sweeter, and though the harsh, urgent sexual energy wasn't as strong, the sweetness was an equally potent lure. But thankfully, the kiss was brief and then he moved back, turning her toward the door and giving her a little push.

"I'll call you. Good night."

She was aware that he waited until she'd turned on some lights before climbing back into his truck. In a minute the growling purr of the engine was lost in the night and all she could hear was the singing of the crickets. As she trailed sleepily through the dark house, all she could think was, *Girl, you are in Trouble.*

Three

***

I'll call you.

In the shower the next morning, she turned her face up to the spray and let it wash away the remnants of a restless night's sleep. Courtesy of one sexy cowboy with the hottest set of lips in the whole state.

After that explosive wrestling match they'd had in his truck, talking on the other end of a telephone line was about as close as she wanted to get to George Deckett Stryker for at least a week.

She spent the day puttering, stenciling a pretty ivy-vine motif in the downstairs bathroom.

Hadn't she learned her lesson? she asked herself as she passed the exit to Wall on the way toward Rapid City later in the afternoon. She sighed. If she wasn't going to repeat the mistakes she'd made back East, the first thing she'd better do was cool it with the cowboys.

Cowboy. Singular. It was a shame all of them weren't

like that obnoxious jerk in the bar yesterday. Cooling it would be no problem then.

Thinking of back East had been a mistake. Her mood took a nosedive. It had been a while since she'd thought of Chet, and she'd liked it that way. Talk about obnoxious jerks. She could still remember the incredulous look on his face when her father had told him her inheritance was tied up in a trust that couldn't be broken. He'd tried to cover it, but within a week he'd broken off their engagement and she'd been left to wonder if there would ever be a man who would look at *her* instead of her family's money.

Her heart skipped a beat as something occurred to her. Deck didn't know about her money, did he? She was fairly sure he only knew her as Cal's kid sister. She took a deep breath as euphoria threatened to sail her right out the window and off into the sky like a helium balloon. Okay, so maybe it was exciting to meet a man who appeared to want her for herself, but that didn't mean she should rush headlong into…into…*bed,* whispered a bad little voice in her head. A relationship, she amended.

Deliberately pushing all thoughts of a certain troublesome cowboy to the back of her mind, she got off the highway at Exit 59 as the postmaster had told her to and stopped at the Rushmore Mall before heading to the hospital. Ninety minutes later she came back to her car and stowed several bags in the hatchback, then went to visit Lyn.

At the door to the room, Silver hesitated, then knocked on the partially open door.

"Come in." The voice was husky, surprisingly musical and distinctly apprehensive.

Silver peeked around the door, smiled and then came the rest of the way into the room. "Hi, Lyn. I'm Silver."

"Hello." Lyn wore a hospital gown and she was propped up against white pillows. The bruises on the young woman's face were even more spectacular colors than yesterday, but she was much cleaner and her long mane of dark-red hair had beautiful copper highlights in it. "Do you remember me?"

Lyn slowly shook her head. "I'm sorry," she said apologetically. "Where have we met?"

"We met yesterday when you knocked on my door."

Lyn's sober expression grew even more so. "I don't remember." She made a small gesture that encompassed her face and body. "Guess this is why."

Silver nodded. "You looked pretty bad yesterday. Scared me silly."

Lyn's wide eyes seemed to take over her face. *Worse than this?* the look seemed to say.

Silver smiled a little. "Deck Stryker helped me get you to the emergency clinic.

"Oh." Lyn cleared her throat. "Did Deck come with you today?"

"No." She was *not* jealous of the way the girl spoke his name as if she knew him well. "But he was here last night. I'm sure he'll be in again."

Lyn made a small negative motion with her head. "He doesn't have to," she said. "It must be horrible for him, coming in here now."

"Why is that? I'm a visitor to the area." *Shame on you, Silver, pumping an injured woman for information.*

"His twin sister was in a car crash when they were in high school," Lyn said. "They brought her here, but she died the next day."

Silver put a hand to her throat. "Dear God. How awful for him."

"It was."

There was a small, awkward silence. She remembered the pallor of Deck's face at both the clinic and the hospital yesterday. He'd been sweating when he walked into the room. She'd assumed it was just too warm for him in the overheated hospital, but now it made more sense. She imagined Cal being killed and her breath caught. Impossible to envision. No wonder the man rarely smiled.

She kept the visit short since the girl clearly was exhausted after just a few minutes. Still, it was getting dark by the time she finally bumped back the lane that led to her brother's house.

She saw the horse before she saw him. It was tied to the fence that ran around the yard, a large dark-colored animal with four white socks that she could see through the gathering dusk. Deck. Who else would be riding over here?

Her pulse picked up. She hadn't expected to see him today, and she wasn't sure she liked the anticipation that flooded her system. It seemed so…needy. And she did not *need* another man cluttering up her life.

Picking up her jacket and her purse, she closed the car door and started across the yard. The dogs came to greet her, one an old yellow mutt with a stiff leg, the other a big and playful younger dog who resembled a collie without a tail more than anything else. Cal had told her both of them were here when he bought the place.

They greeted her with ecstatic wriggling and whining and she stroked their heads as she walked up to the porch. There was a large, dark shadow that looked as if it was wearing a hat sitting in the rocker in the corner. "Hello," she said. "Have you come by for the evening report?"

The shadow stirred and stood, resolving itself into the figure of a tall cowboy. "Among other things," Deck said, striding across the porch toward her.

"You could have gone inside." No way was she going to ask what the "other things" were. "It's chilly out here and Cal says nobody ever locks their doors."

He didn't answer, just stopped a couple of feet away. She could make out his features now and she smiled tentatively, a purely feminine case of the nervous jitters quivering in her stomach. "Want some coffee? A drink? I have iced tea and soda."

"No, thanks." His gaze was on her face, dark and intent, and she found she couldn't sustain the eye contact.

Okay. Well… "I'm going in," she said. "You're welcome to come in. In Virginia, it's warm in May. I'm not used to temperatures near freezing at night."

"Sometimes it's warm here in May, too." Deck followed her into the kitchen. "Last year, it was ninety-six degrees one day while we were branding."

She laughed as she hung her jacket and purse on the hooks inside the door, then turned toward the refrigerator. He might not need a drink, but she was thirsty. "The weather's weird out here."

"Not to us." There was a note of humor in his voice. "Actually, the weather's what I came over here for."

"Oh?"

"You're new." He pointed to the radio Cal had installed under the shelves above the counter the very first day he'd arrived. "Always listen to the weather forecasts. *Always.* There's a stockman's advisory tonight and tomorrow. Possibility of some heavy snow."

"You're kidding." She slowly lowered the glass she'd been drinking from. "Right?"

He shook his head. "Shouldn't be a problem for you since you don't have stock. Don't drive anywhere in the snow. If you have to go somewhere, call over to the house first and let me know. It's not good to be alone out here.

It'll melt fast even if it does snow heavily, but it's best to be prepared.''

It might have been the longest speech she'd heard him make yet. She mentally reviewed his words. Wow—five sentences. But all she said was, ''I'm not used to driving in snow. I won't go anywhere.'' Then she remembered Lyn. ''Rats! I was going to go to the hospital, though.''

Deck shook his head. ''Not if you're not used to driving in lousy weather. Wait until afternoon and I'll drive you over if it's fit.''

''No, I don't want you to have to go back—'' Too late she realized what she was saying. His eyes narrowed fractionally, waiting, and she said lamely, ''Lyn mentioned that you probably didn't like the hospital. She told me about your sister.''

Deck cleared his throat. He suddenly looked remote and untouchable, distant as a star. ''What about her?''

''Just that she died young, in an accident. I'm sorry.'' His eyes were bleak and shadowed, and she had no idea what he was thinking. ''It was stupid of me to bring it up.''

He shrugged, but she could see the pain behind the gesture. ''I'm not big on hospitals, but I'll take you and drop you off if you need me to.''

There was still an open wound here, she thought, a lot more raw than she would have expected after more than a decade. Perhaps it was because they'd been twins. Whatever, it was clear he didn't want to talk about it. ''Thank you. Let's wait and see what tomorrow brings.''

He nodded. ''How's Lyn?''

She tipped her head to one side, considering. ''Healing. Physically, at least. Mentally, I'd imagine it's going to be a while before she feels safe again.''

She finished her tea, rinsed the glass and set it in the

sink, and he straightened from where he'd been lounging against the door frame. They stared at each other, and she could feel the steady pull of attraction willing her to walk across the room to him.

"I have to feed the dogs," she said, forcing herself into motion. She took two bowls from beneath the sink and turned to the pantry where she kept the dog food.

"Silver."

Her hands stilled on the knob of the pantry door. Behind her, heavy footsteps made steady progress across the kitchen. He stopped directly behind her.

"What?" It came out in a hoarse whisper.

Two large hands settled on her shoulders. They were warm and strong, and she swallowed at the first wave of desire that crashed over her head. "Did I imagine it?"

She wasn't stupid. She knew exactly which *it* he meant. "No. But—"

"It's a lousy idea. I know." He moved closer, his breath feathering over her hair, teasing her ear, and she could feel his body heat though he wasn't touching her anywhere but at the point where his hands rested on her shoulders. "We shouldn't get involved."

"No. We—" She stopped, turned to face him. "Why not?" It was one thing for *her* to have reservations but why didn't *he* want *her*?

A gleam of amusement lightened the shadows lingering in his eyes. "I don't need a complication like you in my life."

"Oh." She considered that, decided it was a compliment in a weird sort of way. "Ditto."

But he still had his hands on her shoulders, and as they stared at each other, his hand slipped down her arm and took the bowls from her, setting them aside without ever taking his eyes from her. "A kiss isn't involvement."

"No, definitely not." Her breath was coming in quick little pants. "But it's probably not a good idea."

"I don't care." The words were growled out as he began to lower his head and his hat cast a dark shadow over her face.

As his lips rocked onto hers, his big hands slid from her shoulders to her back, drawing her intimately against him. She couldn't prevent the sound of approval that slipped from her throat at the shock of contact. It was echoed by a masculine groan that vibrated through his mouth and into hers.

She hadn't imagined it, was all she had time to think before she was engulfed. His tongue found hers, surrounded it and drew it into his mouth. His body was big and hard—very hard—and she felt as if his heat was branding her at every point of contact, from her breasts crushed against his chest to the growing erection that pushed insistently against her abdomen. His hands stroked over her shoulders and back and waist and hips as if he were memorizing her body.

Last night he'd been seated but now he stood over and against her, and her breasts ached with arousal. Her nipples drew into hard points so exquisitely painful that every motion of his chest against them elicited fresh streamers of need that flowed directly to the female flesh between her legs, flesh that was already softening and moistening in readiness for what it craved. She shifted her hips against him and gasped when he grasped her bottom and lifted her onto her toes so that his hard shaft fit into the crevice at the top of her thighs.

She was acutely aware of their isolation. They were alone in the house with no chance of an interruption. Her body throbbed and burned for his possession; her common sense turned to ash beneath the white-hot fire he lit within her.

And then he tore his mouth from hers, gasping in harsh, heavy breaths as if he'd just run a marathon. He loosened his grip so that her feet were flat on the floor and threaded his fingers through her hair to palm her skull and press her face into his throat.

"This is insane."

She leaned against him, breathing in his musky, male odor, every limb quaking as she tried to deal with his abrupt withdrawal. He withdrew his arms from around her, and suddenly she knew shame and her cheeks grew hot with it. Both times—last night in the truck and tonight in her kitchen—he'd been the one to call a halt. She'd been all his the moment he touched her, and she was sure he knew it.

Stepping back, she turned her back to him and picked up the dog bowls from where he'd set them on the counter. "It's time for you to leave." She despised the quaver in her voice, and she clamped her lips together.

"Silver, I—"

"*Goodbye.*" She opened the pantry door and stepped inside the small room, waiting for what seemed like forever before his footsteps moved across the floor and she heard her door open and close before his boots stomped off her porch.

She didn't cry over men anymore, she assured herself. Chet had taught her that no man was worth tears, so she resolutely ignored the ache in her throat and the sting in her eyes while she fed the animals. Since it was too early to go to bed she watched television for a while, avoiding anything that smacked remotely of sex or romance, opting for a couple of nature shows and the ten o'clock news.

She couldn't wait till Cal came home so she could tell him what a jerk his next-door neighbor was.

She was the sister of the man who'd killed Genie.
As he reined in his gelding at the barn on the Lucky Stryke, Deck repeated it to himself over and over again like a mantra.

It was the only thing that had kept him from carrying her into her bedroom and stripping her bare so he could get at the long silky body beneath the denim skirt and blouse she'd come home in. He still didn't know why he'd given in to the urge to ride over there tonight. Telling himself he wanted to find out how Lyn was, was a really weak excuse.

God, he was going crazy. He wanted Silver so badly he ached with it. He wanted to kiss those striking eyes closed and plunge into her body until he didn't know where he ended and she began. He wanted her long legs wrapped around his waist and her breasts bared and pink from his handling. He wanted to take her from above and behind and in the shower and in the barn…and he was going to do himself serious injury on this damned horse if he kept thinking about her.

So take her. It would be the perfect revenge. He'd dismissed the thought before.

As bad ideas went, it was the blue-ribbon winner. Low-down and dirty, unworthy as hell.

You can enjoy her and have fun with her. Until her brother comes home. Then he'll put a stop to it and he'll be the one who looks like the bad guy, not you.

It really was a crummy thought, and it made him less of a man than he'd always thought he was. But he *liked* it, dammit. He liked it a lot. He liked the fact that it would give him a reason to pursue the gorgeous package of warm womanhood who'd given him a permanent hard-on since she came to town. He liked the fact that it would royally piss off her brother. And he especially liked the fact that it would drive a wedge between McCall and his sister.

An eye for an eye. He took your sister, you take his.

And as he thought about that, all reservations about seducing Silver vanished beneath a steely determination and sweet relief. She was going to be his. And he was going to take her and use her until he tired of her, and then her brother could have her back. At least he'd give him that, he thought bitterly. *I didn't get my sister back.*

Unbidden, memories of that final night of Genie's life wormed their way into his mind while he stabled the horse. He'd had nightmares for years, but they'd come less and less frequently as time passed. It almost frightened him. He never wanted to forget her.

Deliberately he called up images from that night. Moment after moment rolled across his mental screen and he welcomed them, using the grim reminder to assure himself that his plan was just.

The first memory to come was Cal's laughing face as he'd pulled his daddy's new pickup to a halt in front of the Stryker house that night. He and Genie had raced outside and piled in, calling goodbyes to their parents with the blithe unconcern of youth. *See you. We'll be back later.*

The second was the dance, followed by the fight that had sidelined Cal.

And then the accident.

For years he'd had dreams in which McCall died horribly, dreams in which a judge banged an enormous gavel and sentenced the killer to the life term he deserved, dreams in which he, Deck, smashed his fists into McCall's shocked face again and again and again, until he was less recognizable than Genie had been in her final moments. There was little he could think of that would satisfy him more in this life than to find a way to take revenge on the man who'd killed his twin sister.

If not for McCall, she'd probably be happily married by now, mothering children and loving some lucky guy. She'd still be riding, roping, racing. Automatically his gaze traveled to the corner stall near the door where the little paint mare she'd so loved still resided. Who'd have ever thought the horse would outlive her owner?

And who would have thought Cal McCall would have the guts to come back to Kadoka, even after all these years? He'd left only weeks after coming home from the hospital that summer and he'd never been back. Deck had never known where he went and he'd never cared. If McCall hadn't come back, hadn't bought the place next door and shoved himself right in the town's face again, he'd have been nothing more than a bad memory for the rest of Deck's life.

But he had come back. And he still had to pay.

Revenge had been an amorphous, half-formed imagining for over a dozen years. But now, with McCall's return, was it possible that revenge could become reality?

His heart hardened to a block of stone as he decided it could.

It *would*.

Two evenings later Deck raised one booted foot and propped it on the crossbar beneath the small, sturdy wooden table where he'd settled in for a Friday-night drink an hour ago. They hadn't gotten the snow they'd expected, and the inch or two they had gotten was already a greasy gumbo with puddles everywhere you looked.

And he hadn't seen Silver since the evening he'd ridden away from her. It had been a long two days. Only because he couldn't wait to start his seduction of Cal McCall's sister.

The door opened and banged shut again. Deck shoved out the chair opposite him, maintaining his carefully balanced position on the back two legs of his own seat. The other chair teetered for a moment before a man's hand grabbed the back. Beer sloshed over the rim of the full mug on the table as Marty folded himself onto the chair's seat.

Marty removed his dun-colored hat and tossed it carelessly on the table. He reached for Deck's drink and downed a healthy slug.

"Hey!" Deck protested. "Get your own."

His brother grinned. "In a minute." Then the waitress scurried over and he ordered a draft beer.

"Hey, Marty. You trying to keep Deck outta trouble?"

"Yep. It's a full-time job, Lula May."

The buxom little blonde chuckled, winking at Deck with exaggerated intimacy. "Don't I know it."

Deck didn't bother to smile. Rumor went that Lula May Piersen had been in the sack with half the men in Jackson County. He wasn't one of them and he intended to keep it that way.

"Hey, Lula, when you going to marry me?" Marty had an ease with women, a natural instinct for flirting with anything female, that Deck had never picked up. Mostly because he didn't need to. When he wanted a woman, there was usually one around ready to scratch his itch. The rest of the time he was more than content to talk to the animals with whom he spent much of each day.

Or at least he had been until Silver Jenssen had sashayed into town.

And as with every other time he'd thought of her in the past couple of days, he formed a carefully detailed picture of his sister's broken body. Cal deserved whatever he got.

Lula May arched a brow in wry amusement as she hefted her drink tray. "Marty Stryker, there're a lot of things I'd be glad to do with you but marrying isn't one of 'em. No way do I want to be stepmama to that little firecracker of a daughter of yours." And with one final flirtatious smile, she headed back to the bar.

Marty shook his head and heaved a mock sigh. "Damn. Struck out again."

Deck grunted. "I'd like to see your face if she'd said yes."

Marty hooted, giving him an exaggerated leer. "So would I." Then his grin faded, and he rubbed a hand over his stubbled jaw. "I did something kind of crazy today."

"Just today?"

"Jerk." Marty pulled a crumpled scrap of paper from his pocket and used the tip of his index finger to flick it across the table at Deck. "Put this in the papers in Rapid City and Pierre."

Deck unfolded the sheet of paper and squinted at Marty's poor excuse for handwriting. "'S-W-M, 30s,'" he read. He stopped and glanced at his brother. "What is this, some kind of code? A new brand of motor oil?"

"No, you idiot." Marty shook his head. "It's an advertisement." Reaching across the table, he plucked the ad out of Deck's fingers.

"Single white male, thirties," he read. "Prosperous rancher seeks hardworking woman for marriage, household management, child care. Offers security, fidelity and comfortable life-style."

A rusty chuckle worked its way up and rumbled out before Deck could catch it back. "You're advertising for a *wife?*'' The chuckle threatened to become a full-fledged howl of mirth.

A dark-bronze color was climbing from the neck of Marty's work shirt. ''Don't see what's so wrong with that,'' he said with stiff defensiveness. ''I don't have time for courting, and we aren't close enough to a decent-size town for me to meet many women.''

Deck shook his head, still trying not to give in to the laughter that threatened. ''I may not read the papers,'' he said, ''but even I know there isn't a woman on earth who's going to read that ad and leap to answer it. You might as well hire a housekeeper and a nanny.''

''Don't want a housekeeper,'' Marty retorted. ''I want a wife.'' His cheeks flushed even more. ''I'm tired of sleeping alone.''

''There's ways to fix that without marrying,'' Deck advised his elder brother.

''Easy for you to say.'' Marty surveyed him sourly. ''You didn't let another man even get a chance at an introduction to Silver McCall.''

''Jenssen. Her last name is Jenssen.''

''Who cares what her last name is?''

Deck propped his elbows on the table and plunged his fingers into the thick mess of curls that quirked over his forehead. Quietly he lifted his head and looked across the table at Marty. ''I don't,'' he said. ''She's kin to Cal McCall. That's good enough for me.''

Something in his tone made Marty glance at him with narrow suspicion in his blue eyes. ''You're not thinking of doing something stupid, are you?''

''No.'' He was sure of that. McCall deserved this.

''That doesn't exactly ring with truth,'' Marty commented. He raised a troubled gaze to meet Deck's.

"There's no law that says McCall can't come around here. He's not guilty of anything."

"Legally."

"Or otherwise," his brother said sharply.

"To you."

"And the rest of the world." Marty heaved a sigh, staring into his beer. "Yeah, I was mad enough to kill him for a while, too. But once the anger faded, I faced facts. It was an *accident*. Deck—" his voice grew quiet "—You've got to get past the anger someday." A long silence hung behind his words. Memories heavy with sorrow wrapped the two men in a morose camaraderie.

Marty was wrong. Deck knew it as surely as he knew his own name. McCall *was* responsible.

But he'd be sorry, Deck reminded himself, and the moment would be sweet. After all these years he'd have a small taste of how it felt to have a sister ripped out of your heart.

Four

The rodeo. Silver skirted the horses and their young riders as she made her way around the ring to the far side, where covered bleachers were provided for spectators. It was a glorious June day, not too hot, certainly not too cold, and she was planning to enjoy herself.

Cal had intended to bring her to this, but when he'd been called away she'd decided to go, anyway. Who knew how long she'd be in South Dakota and if she'd have another chance to see a rodeo? His directions to the rodeo in Wall had been easy to follow and here she was.

It was kind of nice being anonymous. She didn't exactly fit in with her white tennis sneakers; she supposed she'd have to get some boots. Maybe she'd stop over at the Wall Drugstore, which loudly proclaimed itself the largest in the world. Strictly speaking, it wasn't a drugstore. It was more like a conglomeration of specialty shops, everything from jewelry to Western wear to books to tourist junk. Cal had brought her into Wall on the way to Kadoka her first day here just to show her the street-long storefront.

Silver sat alone in the stands for a short time. Then a woman a few feet away said hello. When she learned Silver was new to the area, she made it a personal mission to educate her in the ways of the rodeo.

Calf roping for cowgirls meant lassoing the calf by the horns while the men had to catch a hind leg with their loop. Calf wrestling was as muddy as it sounded. She felt sorry for the frightened-looking calves that were sent into the ring for roping and wrestling but knew better than to say so.

Bronc riding was interesting and exciting while bull riding made her heart leap into her throat and stay there while a defenseless cowboy tried to stay on the bull for eight long seconds. She didn't breathe while those who got thrown scrambled to avoid being gored or trampled until they could get out of the ring and the rodeo clowns brazenly distracted the angry animal. It didn't make her feel any better when the woman related stories of teenagers paralyzed by being slammed against a gate by a bull, and the professional rodeo cowboy who was gored in the ring and died on the spot.

But it all was fascinating. Some of the people around her seemed to share her reluctant mesmerized attention, while others screamed and cheered for their relatives. Children played, mothers chased them, men stood in small clumps and talked. Some things didn't change no matter where a person went.

Finally, as the bull riding drew its final few contestants of the day, she decided it was time to head home before she got caught in the parking lot with a hundred stock trailers. After offering her garrulous companion a warm thanks, she started toward the parking lot. A little concessions trailer stood on her right as she continued toward the parking lot and she decided to get a hot dog and a soda. After all, it was almost suppertime.

As she threaded her way between groups of jean jackets and cowboy hats toward the food wagon, she kept her head down. She imagined that this place was like most other largely male enclaves around the world, and a single woman could attract more attention than she wanted without much effort.

She was almost there when a hand curled around her elbow. "Good afternoon."

Her heart did one quick back-flip as she recognized the voice, and she jerked fiercely at her elbow, but the fingers were an inflexible prison. "Let me go," she demanded in a low voice.

"I want to talk to you." Deck was freshly showered and shaved, and as always he wore the black hat. Beneath its brim, his eyes were a deep, stormy blue as he looked down at her from his superior height, and he quickly maneuvered her to the edge of the crowd where the rows of vehicles began to fill up an adjacent field.

He planted himself in front of her with his back to the rodeo crowd, a dark angel with the devil in his eyes. She remembered the feel of his hands on her body and felt a treacherous thrill shoot through her. And then she remembered the way he'd backed off, as if she'd had the plague, and the thrill died away to a hurtful throb. Fresh pain poured out of the wound he'd made. Obviously, he wasn't happy about the attraction that leaped between them, and she had no intention of pushing herself at a man who didn't like the fact that he wanted her.

"I don't want to talk to you." She concentrated on keeping her legs from shaking.

Deck didn't smile, although his eyes warmed and one side of his mouth quirked. "And she's subtle, too, folks."

Silver didn't answer him. She hadn't expected to see him here. That was all it was. If she'd been prepared, he never would have shaken her composure like this.

But as she ducked around him and headed for the crowd again, Deck snagged her wrist in one large hand. "Stay here for a minute."

His palm was hard and callused, warm and oddly gentle, though she doubted she could get free unless he chose to let her go. His thumb slipped slowly down to rub a light, circular pattern over the sensitive flesh on her inner wrist, and she had a sudden vivid memory of him holding her gaze with his as he kissed her there. She shivered, but when she tugged at her hand she found she was right. He had no intention of letting her go.

She didn't want to make a scene in front of all the strangers who were beginning to cast sideways glances at them, so instead of the response that sprang to her lips, she forced herself to say, "All right. But let's go farther away. I don't like being part of the entertainment."

He nodded and started to lead her through the parking lot. But to her chagrin he didn't let her go. She glanced up at him, ready to make a light comment about getting her hand back, but the sensual set of his firm lips in profile made her forget whatever she'd been going to say. Those lips had moved on hers the other night, and the feelings they'd generated inside her were enough to make her spontaneously combust.

"I'm not trying to run away." As he rushed her through the parking lot, Silver lifted the wrist he had shackled with his fingers. "You can let me go now."

Deck looked down at her. "I don't think so." But as he pulled her arm back down, his fingers slipped away from her wrist and he laced them through hers in an intimate, if more conventional, handclasp.

There was no use arguing. She already knew him well enough to know he had a bullheaded streak a mile wide. So she pretended that the flesh connection of their fingers wasn't making her pulse skitter around and her breathing quicken as if she'd just run a sprint.

Finally they stopped beside his black pickup. He walked her around to the passenger side and opened the door. "Get in."

"Get in? Where are we going?"

"I'm driving you home."

"Oh, no, you're not. I drove my brother's truck here."

"You can get it tomorrow. Ride home with me tonight."

She was nearly speechless at the man's gall. After the way he'd treated her— "After the way you treated me the other night you expect me to just hop in your truck and ride the whole way home with you? I don't think so."

Deck pivoted to face her. "I'm sorry for that," he said in a low voice. "I...don't really know why I did it."

"It doesn't matter." She deliberately left her hand limp and kept her eyes downcast.

His hand tightened around hers. "It does to me." His voice was deep and quiet. Sincere.

Chet had seemed sincere, too, and look where *that* had gotten her. She refused to look up at him, to respond.

But he had ways around that. In the late-day's light, he stepped closer, reaching down to take her other hand in his, as well. "It's never been like this for me. Can you say you don't feel it, too?"

No. She *couldn't* say that. And what's more, she suspected he knew it. Finally she looked up at him, barely able to see his features beneath the deeper shadow of his hat. "I feel it," she whispered. "But that doesn't mean I want to pursue it."

"One chance," he said. "Just one more chance."

In one more chance, he could break your heart, said the voice of self-preservation inside her head.

But as she hesitated, he released one hand and brought his own up beneath her chin. With a large, gentle finger, he tilted her face up, inspecting her features in the evening's weak light. His face looked drawn and desperate, and the wave of longing that swept through her urged her to set her fears aside, to give herself to this man who wanted her, to comfort him and erase the sadness in the depths of his eyes.

"All right." She closed her eyes as she said it, not sure she wanted to examine the decision too closely.

And then she felt the hot lick of his breath over her cheek, the warm shock of his lips touching hers, trailing over her jaw to the sensitive spot behind her ear. Her body tightened but before she could respond, he drew away. "Thank you."

"I still don't want to leave the truck here." It was a small thing, but to her it was important. She was totally alone here until Cal returned. If she didn't have transportation and Deck couldn't or wouldn't bring her back to get the truck, she'd be in a jam. Just as she was realizing that her reluctance indicated she still didn't trust his change of heart, Deck nodded.

"That's okay. If you want to follow me, there's a little restaurant in Wall where we can stop."

So she followed the black truck out of the rodeo field through Wall. The place he took her was a nice little family-style restaurant very different from the bar they'd gone into the other day.

At Deck's request, the hostess placed them at a quiet

table in a corner. Once he'd seated her, he removed his hat and took a seat at her left hand with his back to the room. "So what did you think of the rodeo?"

"It was…interesting. I'm still trying to figure out why anyone would want to ride a bull."

He shrugged. "It's a real rush, pitting yourself against one of those big boys."

"Until you get trampled."

He shrugged. "The ones who stay with it are pretty good at watching out for themselves."

"Have you ever tried it?"

He nodded. "A couple of times. Guess I'm just not crazy enough. Bronc riding, on the other hand, is a whole lot of fun."

His jaw was stubbled with golden bristles that framed his lips. She caught herself watching his mouth as he formed his words, drowning common sense in the movement of that full, reddened flesh that curved and quirked so enticingly. Her palms itched, and she closed her fingers into fists in her lap to keep from reaching out and tracing the shape of his upper lip with her finger.

When his large hand descended on hers, she jumped a foot in her chair. She raised her gaze to his, stunned by the need rolling through her at the simple touch of his hard, rough hand enclosing her smaller, fisted one. He lifted it onto the table, toying with it as his eyes held hers. "What are you thinking?"

She shook her head. "Stupid thoughts. Very stupid thoughts."

A chuckle worked its way up and out of his chest. "Sometimes those are the best kind."

She didn't want to engage in this little game of sexual innuendo with him, not when her whole body quivered at his nearness and her heart raced at the mere touch of his hand. ''Sometimes they're not,'' she said quietly.

Turning her head, she looked out the plate-glass window that formed part of the corner behind them. The restaurant was on the edge of town, and she had an unobstructed view of the broad, rolling prairie. ''That's so beautiful,'' she said.

To her relief he accepted the change of subject. ''I think so, too. Some people hate it, though. Your mother, from what I hear, found it too big and too desolate.''

She nodded. ''Mama's a city girl at heart. And she missed having her family five minutes away.'' She shook her head. ''She says her libido ran away with her common sense when she married Tom McCall and she must be right. I can't imagine any other reason my mother would have come out here.''

''Women who aren't raised out here often find it too primitive and isolated.''

Silver shrugged. ''It hasn't bothered me so far, although I've hardly been here long enough to know. But I don't think I'd mind it. There's a very different sort of beauty out here—the wide-open space is very appealing. I love the way the sky seems so blue, the mountains way off in the distance, being able to see for miles.''

''That comes in handy in tornado weather,'' he said wryly as the waitress approached and began to list the specials.

While they were waiting for their meals to arrive, she said, ''Tell me about your ranch.''

He looked a little blank. ''What do you want to know?''

''What kind of outfit is it? That's the correct word, right?''

"Yeah." One corner of his lips rose in the now-familiar half smile. "Cow-calf."

She nodded. "I think that's what Cal plans to start, too."

"That's what his daddy did." Deck didn't elaborate, but then, she didn't expect him to. The fact that they were exchanging unlimited consecutive sentences was miracle enough for her.

"What kind of cattle do you raise?"

He raised an eyebrow. "How many times have you driven past my fences?"

She grinned. "That doesn't mean I know what kind of cow is standing on the other side. Let's see, Holstein, Brahma, Heifer—"

He was struggling not to laugh, she could tell. "A Holstein is usually a dairy cow. Brahma are run down toward the south, around Texas and New Mexico, because they do well in real dry areas. And a heifer isn't a breed of cow. It's a name for a female cow."

"Oh." She considered. "So what kind do you have?"

"Angus. Black Angus, although every once in a while one'll throw a red hide."

She blinked. "Meaning?"

"Red is a recessive color for Angus. Occasionally we'll get a red calf from a black cow and bull."

"You don't have any Longhorns, I notice. See, I *do* know something about cattle."

He almost smiled that time. The corners of his eyes crinkled and she could see twin flames of merriment dancing in the blue depths. "We don't like Longhorns. They're hardy but they have a cantankerous nature. A lot of 'em are just flat-out mean. And the cows get real feisty when they have calves running around." He shook his head. "The outfit on the other side of ours runs Longhorn.

I've had words with that guy about keeping his bulls away from my cows.''

Apparently there were a few topics on which Deck would speak in full sentences, she thought, hiding a smile. "You mean his bulls get onto your land."

Deck gave a disgusted snort. "They get onto more than just my land.''

"Oh.'' She could feel her cheeks growing warm. But if she was going to spend any time out here, she was going to have to get used to the blunt discussions of animal husbandry that could be overheard nearly everywhere a person went. "I guess crossbreeding isn't a good thing.''

"Depends on the breeds you're working with. Longhorn crosses are hard on Angus cows,'' he said. "So are Charolais. The calves have large heads and often the births are hard.''

"When are calves born?'' she asked.

"Springtime,'' he said. "Generally middle of March, except for a few late calvers.'' He grimaced. "And there'll be a few early ones if that damned Longhorn bull was in with the cattle for very long.''

"How old are the calves when you brand them?''

His eyebrows rose. "About two months. Marty and I are going to be branding late calves next week. I'd invite you to watch, but it's pretty nasty.''

"I don't mind. Would it bother you if I came over?''

He hesitated and an oddly blank look came over his face. Then he shook his head. "No. If you can stomach it, you're welcome. I might even put you to work.'' He paused. "Why so many questions? You thinking about going into the business?''

She smiled. "It's a little embarrassing to be so ignorant of my own brother's life. I'm trying to get a picture of what Cal was like as a child. You know, his background, the things that were a part of his upbringing. It's very different in Virginia."

"Did you live there all your life?"

"Yes. Daddy's family has been in Albemarle County for generations."

"Any other brothers or sisters?"

She shook her head. "Just Cal. But I have a lot of cousins on Daddy's side, and there are several near my age that lived close by when I was growing up. I wasn't lonely."

"I've never been East," he said. "What's the land like?"

"Mountainous," she said. "With lots of trees. Out here you can see for miles. At home there are lots of rolling hills. The mountains are old and worn down. And there are a whole lot more people per square inch."

"How about water?"

She laughed. "Trust a rancher to think about water. Yes, there's water. Streams, rivers, springs, creeks, an ocean a few hours away...."

"You've seen the ocean?" He seemed surprised.

"If you live on the East Coast, chances are good you've been to the ocean."

"I'd like to see the ocean someday," he said. The waitress came over with their food, a steak for Deck and a cheeseburger platter for Silver, and the conversation slowed as they ate.

Walking across the parking lot afterward, Deck reached for her hand. "How about if I follow you home?"

She thought for a moment. When she met his eyes, she saw a raw, hot wanting that echoed her own, and the feeling shook her right down into her tennis shoes. "No," she said. "That would not be smart."

He laughed, but it was a sound of frustration more than humor. "No, it wouldn't be. Let's live dangerously."

She shook her head. "Sorry. I've had my share of danger. I'm looking for safe and comfortable these days."

His mouth thinned into a flat line. "Silver, I haven't felt *comfortable* since the day you fetched up against me in the grocery store. I can guaran-damn-tee you that you and I aren't going to be *comfortable* together." His lips tilted into a sideways smile. "At least not until we're both too exhausted to move."

His words brought mental images she'd rather not have slipping through her mind. Did he have any idea how badly she wanted him?

Probably, she decided, noting the glint in his eye. Still, she just didn't think—

"As for safe," he said, "isn't it better to take a chance sometimes when the reward might be worth it?"

She looked away from his compelling gaze, swallowing the words of acquiescence that tried to spill from her throat. "I don't know," she said softly. He was still holding her hand, and she looked down at their linked fingers. The contrast between his big, dark hand and her own much smaller, pale and slender fingers was marked. It suddenly seemed far more intimate than a simple handclasp, and that sensation of her muscles contracting sizzled its way through her again.

He must have felt something, because his hand tightened around hers. "All right," he said. "How about a ride tomorrow? I have to move some cattle in the morning, but later I have to check fences. Would you like to come along?"

She turned it over in her head but couldn't see any obvious flaws. On horseback they would be far enough apart to keep her from jumping his bones despite her better judgment. "All right," she said. "Why do you move cows?"

"Good grass," he said. Then, when she waited, he added, "They're in the smaller winter pasture but this group has older calves that were all branded two weeks ago and it's time to move them down to the base of the butte."

"Ah." She nodded. "You do realize I'll probably drive you crazy with questions."

He chuckled. Then he shifted, releasing her hand and sliding his big, rough palms loosely around her waist as he brought her to face him. "I might need some incentive to keep me talking."

"Incentive," she repeated, feeling bold. They were in a parking lot—again. What could happen? Granted, it wasn't exactly swarming with people, and dusk was rapidly giving way to full dark, but she felt safe enough here. "And what might I have that you'd take in trade?"

He moved closer, his hat blocking out the starry sky overhead, and his hands pulled her up against him so that her body was flush against the hot, solid length of his. "This," he said as he kissed her.

His tongue should be illegal, she thought hazily as he plumbed the soft warmth of her mouth. Or marked with a big yellow Caution sign, at the very least. As he nipped his way along the line of her jaw to suck her earlobe into his mouth and use that tongue on it, she shuddered, her body so hot and electric she thought she might burst into flames.

She whimpered, a little sound of please-more-again ecstasy, and his hands moved, one sliding down her bottom to cup a buttock and squeeze gently, his big fingers slipping a little way into the sensitive crease of her bottom and making her buck against him. The other boldly marched over her hip and up the front of her torso to cup her breast and she gasped at the heat that surrounded her. He rubbed a thumb relentlessly back and forth over the fabric of her blouse until she felt her nipple draw into a tight bud that shot lightning bolts of hot sexual need zinging straight to her womb. Wrapping her arms around his neck, she pushed herself up on her toes, trapping the steely bulge at his groin against her belly.

He groaned and came back to devour her mouth, but some remnant of common sense trickled into her mind and she dragged one hand from the back of his neck. Hastily she thrust it between them, over his mouth.

"Wait," she whispered.

"Don't want to," he muttered against her palm, using his tongue to draw little swirly circles right in the sensitive center of her hand.

"We're standing in a *parking lot,*" she reminded him, snatching her hand away.

The heavy muscles in his arms tightened for a moment, and she had a second of panic. Then his arms relaxed, and she didn't know whether to be thankful or cry when he pulled back and put a little space between them. "A parking lot won't do for what I have in mind," he informed her.

She swallowed at the hot intent in his eyes and she dipped her head, resting her forehead against his broad chest. "I don't think I'm ready for what you have in mind."

He rubbed his hands down her back, wisely refraining from comment. "I'll come over after lunch tomorrow and take you riding with me." He paused for a second and she looked up at him. "Uh, you do ride, right?"

A bubble of laughter threatened and she almost said No just to see the look on his face. "I ride," she confirmed.

"But I rode English until last week. Cal took me out in a Western saddle."

"Good," he said. "It's a better way to ride."

She raised her eyebrows. "Says you."

"You go skidding down a steep slope or try to stay on a horse that's gotten spooked by a snake, and then tell me you'd rather be in one of those flimsy little saddles," he said.

"I'd rather be—"

"Smart-ass," he growled. He bent his knees and pressed a hard kiss to her lips, then dropped his hands and stepped clear away from her. "I'll bring a horse for you." Then he turned her and pointed her in the direction of her brother's truck, slapping her on the rump like a fractious mare. "Now get out of here while I'm still inclined to let you go."

She opened her mouth to make another flip comment but the light of battle gleaming in his eye just dared her to utter it. Hastily she shut her mouth. The last thing she needed was to be tossed over his shoulder and dragged off to his lair to be ravished.

Even if the thought was a secret delight.

So she went, getting into Cal's truck and driving out of the parking lot after giving him an easy wave. He wasn't far behind her the whole way back to Kadoka, and it wasn't until he turned off the highway onto his own ranch's gravel lane that she breathed a sigh of relief. She hadn't been at all sure that the big black truck wasn't going to follow her right on home.

Her lane was next, and she drove the miles back to the house, realizing as she did so how dark and lonely it was out here. The dogs who came out from beneath the bushes near the porch to greet her were a welcome sight.

Inside, the answering machine light blinked. She

punched the replay button and after a moment her brother's voice filled the room.

"Hey, Silver. Sorry I missed you. Where the heck are you, anyway, at eight o'clock in the evening? I don't imagine there are too many hot dates hanging around Jackson County."

You couldn't be more wrong, big brother.

"Anyway, I'll try to call in a day or so. Looks like I have about a week's worth of stuff to do before I come home. Let me know if you don't want to stay that long. I won't blame you if you don't. I know living on a ranch in the ass end of nowhere all alone wasn't what you came to South Dakota for." Her brother rattled off the number where he was staying in case she needed to reach him and hung up.

Darn! She was sorry she'd missed him. She had lots to tell him: about Lyn, for one thing, and Deck, for another. Maybe she'd give him a call tomorrow evening.

"Where're you taking—" Marty's eyes widened at the sight of Deck leading the little paint mare out of the barn the next day.

Deck sighed. Why did Marty have to come out here at this exact moment? Two more minutes and he'd have been gone. "I'm riding fence this afternoon," he said.

"I know." His brother raised one eyebrow. "Since when do you need two horses to do it?"

"Since I invited Silver to ride along," Deck growled.

Marty's eyes widened. "You invited— And you're going to put her on Genie's horse?"

"She doesn't get ridden enough," Deck said defensively. "We're too heavy for her."

"I didn't say I minded." Marty took off his hat and

lightly slapped it against his leg, but his sky-blue eyes watched Deck the whole time. "You like her?"

Deck knew he wasn't talking about the horse. "She's hot," he said dismissively, then felt a twinge of shame at the way he'd made Silver sound cheap and easy.

Marty scratched his head slowly. "Well," he said, "If she's that hot, maybe I should be the one to take her riding."

The graphic suggestion Deck made had Marty hooting with laughter, but the laughter faded after a moment. Marty squinted in the bright sunlight as he looked up at the seated horseman. "You don't really want to do this," he said slowly. "She's Cal's sister."

"That's exactly why I want to do this."

Marty's eyes were worried. He fondled the ears of his Australian cattle dog, Streak, with an absent hand as he watched Deck turn the horses and ride out of the barn. Then he shrugged. "Don't do anything I wouldn't do."

"I'd be bored in ten minutes if I listened to that."

Deck took a fairly direct route to the McCall outfit, inspecting the line of fences as he went. Once he crossed onto McCall land, he didn't stop the inspection. Cal had a bit of work to do before he could run cattle, he reflected. Old man Hamill hadn't done squat to take care of the fences in his last few years.

Still, the alfalfa was a good size, and it smelled of the twin scents of mustard and lavender, a sickly odor that reminded him vaguely of old socks. Wildflowers dotted the pastures once he got away from the alfalfa field, and in a little draw where a creek ran in a good summer, the smell of the currant bushes surrounded him.

After a steady thirty minutes he came over the knob to see the McCall house down on the flat plane below. It was a pretty, old farmhouse, even if it had been let go in the past few years. Yes, indeed, Cal was going to have his hands full trying to turn himself from a fancy-pants city boy into a rancher again.

He rode right down to her yard like he had the other night and tied both horses to the posts of the fence by the walk. In another couple of weeks, the wild rambler roses that grew on the fence would be smothered with blooms. He hadn't been over here in years—were they still the little pink ones from his childhood or had the bush been replaced?

The two dogs came to greet him, the old one walking so stiffly he winced as he bent to scratch the poor old guy's neck.

"Hello."

When he glanced up, she was standing behind the screen door, framed in its upper panel. "Hi." He had to clear his throat after uttering the simple word; every damn time he saw her again she took his breath away. As she opened the door and stepped onto the porch, desire slammed into him so hard his knees felt weak.

She wore jeans again today, with a pale-pink shirt and a fleece-lined denim vest that should have covered up her assets but only hugged her curves in a way that made his eyes keep straying back for a second peek. Her curly hair flew around her face, and in one hand she carried a buff-colored hat which she held up with a doubtful expression. "Cal bought me this before he left. I don't quite picture myself as a cowgirl, but if you think I need it, I'll wear it." She paused. "I guess."

"Wear it. The sun gets pretty fierce sometimes and there's not a lot of shade around here to hide in, in case you didn't notice." He gestured to the dog at his side. "Your brother ought to take this guy in to the vet if he's planning to let him hang around. There are a couple of new arthritis medicines that work pretty well."

She nodded as if she liked the idea. "The man who came out to work on the plumbing last week said Cal ought to just shoot him."

He liked the indignant tone in her voice. "There are a lot of folks who think like that out here," he told her. "If a dog isn't good for something, they don't spend the money."

"That's terrible."

He lifted a shoulder. "That's economics. Ranching's not an easy life or one that will make you rich. Vets are an expensive luxury for people who are wondering how they'll pay the feed bill next month. Chances are, this old boy was welcome at somebody's outfit until he got too old to work." Then he straightened. "You ready to go for a ride?"

She smiled. "You betcha."

"Are you trying to turn yourself into a local?" He found himself smiling back. "I know darn well they don't say that in Virginia."

She laughed. "No, they don't. If someone asked me that in Virginia, I might have said, 'I sure am, honey.'"

He gave a snort of laughter. "Spoken like a true Southern belle."

"I hope you'll go easy on this Southern belle today. It's been a while since I've been on a horse." As she spoke, she handed him a wrapped package to put into the saddlebags his gelding wore. "Snacks."

He accepted the food and stored it as he considered her words. "How long a while?"

She shot him a rueful smile as she tugged the new hat firmly into place. "Oh, five years, give or take a few, since I rode with any regularity."

He whistled. "Riding fence might not be the best way to reintroduce you."

But she shook her head. "I'll be fine. I've been looking forward to getting out of the house all day."

She swung into the saddle gracefully and his pulse jumped into a faster rhythm as her jeans stretched tight across a trim bottom for a moment until she settled into the big saddle. "Okay," she said. "I'm ready."

He took her out past the winter pastures on McCall land toward the White River, where they crossed and then rode along the river bottom to the fences that went over east. For about forty minutes they rode across prairie.

She sniffed appreciatively when they passed a big patch of wildflowers. "That smells wonderful. What is it?"

"It's a couple of different kinds of wildflowers," he told her. "Phlox, larkspur, daisies, wild sweet william, sego lilies…"

She was instantly diverted. "Is that where your horse got its name?"

He nodded.

"How about mine? Lindra's unusual."

He couldn't answer her for a moment and he looked away, through the cottonwoods and plums and thickets of chokecherry. "My sister named her," he finally said. "She made it up."

There was a moment of silence. The odd, sad calls of curlews overhead and the jingle of the bridles as the horses plodded along suddenly seemed much louder.

"I'm sorry." Silver's voice was low and subdued. "I didn't want to remind you of sad things."

He shrugged. "You didn't know." *But your brother does.* The thought reminded him of the reason this partic-ular woman was riding with him and of what he planned to do. Closing his mind to any voice of caution, he said,

"Why don't we take a little break? There's a good little patch of shade up ahead in the windbreak. We can let the horses rest, too." The windbreak was one of many stands of pines his mother had planted during her life on the ranch.

"What's a windbreak?"

He pointed to the pines they were approaching. "Those didn't grow there naturally. We plant them on purpose, to give the cattle a place to shelter during storms. Snow will pile up against a little hill or a copse of trees and the cattle huddle on the other side where it's more protected. A good windbreak can save a whole herd of cows during a blizzard."

Silver nodded, leaning forward in her saddle for a better look. "Were these planted in your lifetime?"

"Yes. It was my mother's pet project. She used to order a couple hundred little pines every year and plant 'em in triple rows wherever Dad thought they'd work best."

"That's a wonderful idea." Her voice was warm. "If I come to visit Cal next year, maybe I'll plan to come in May again so I can do the same thing on his land."

They reached the pines and Deck dismounted. As Silver did the same, he opened the saddlebag Sego carried and withdrew the blanket he'd stashed. He carried the blanket into the shadow cast by the copse of pines and spread it out on the fragrant carpet of needles in the shady spot. From the other pack, he took a big canteen and the packages Silver had handed him back at the house. Then he gestured to the blanket. "Have a seat."

She walked to the blanket and lowered herself in one smooth motion, leaning back on her hands and stretching her legs before her. "It's a beautiful day."

"It is," he agreed, lowering himself beside her in a similar position. The way she sat thrust her breasts against the soft fabric of the pink shirt and outlined the flat planes of her hips and belly, and he tried not to stare. "It was seventy-eight degrees when I left to ride over to your place. If that isn't just about perfect, I don't know what is."

She reached for the package she'd brought along. "Want a cookie?"

The cookies she'd made were the chocolate kind his mother had called no-bakes because they got cooked atop the stove. His mouth watered. "I think I'm in Heaven. This is one of my favorite kinds."

"I like them, too. I had a chocolate craving—that's why I made them."

He took a cookie and bit into it. "Mmmm. I haven't had these in ages. Since Mom moved to Florida, probably. I can barely boil water, and my brother isn't exactly what you'd call a gourmet chef."

She laughed, and the light sound danced out across the prairie grasses as she leaned back again, this time on her elbows. "I like to cook but I'd hardly classify myself as a gourmet."

"You can cook for me anytime."

Her eyebrows rose. "Wow. Now there's an offer I can't refuse." Her voice held a gentle irony. The full Cupid's bow of her lips quirked in a smile again, and as their eyes met, he felt the white heat of sexual attraction sear him from the inside out. Abruptly he decided it was time to do something about it.

Rolling to his side, he tugged her elbow out from under her and trapped her beneath him. He leaned over her, his weight against her hip, and in her eyes he saw the instant she realized what he intended.

"Deck, I—"

"Shhh. Don't talk." He leaned closer, sliding his free hand across her stomach, feeling the muscles quiver beneath his hand. "Just enjoy."

Five

Silver didn't move for a long moment. Above her the dark branches of the pines were outlined against a sky so bright and blue it didn't look real. Deck's head and broad shoulders blocked much of her view and as she stared up at his fallen-angel features, a half-smile lifted one corner of his mouth.

"Relax," he said. "This isn't going to hurt."

"How do you know?" It was intended to be saucy and flippant, but even she heard the quaver in her voice.

"Because something that feels this good can't hurt." His voice was soothing. He spread his palm wide where it rested across her midriff, and she couldn't prevent an involuntary intake of breath at the sensations that radiated from his touch.

She studied his face, watching him as his gaze followed the movement of his hand. His jaw was long and square, bristling with gleaming stubble that echoed the color of the thick, wavy hair she knew was hidden beneath his hat.

As if he'd divined her thoughts, his hand went to his hat, sweeping it off and tossing it aside, then flipping hers over to land atop it.

"We don't need these in the shade," he told her in a deep, rough voice.

She knew what he expected, what he intended. His eyes were a deep, impenetrable blue as he awaited her reaction, and he held himself so still above her that she could feel the tension quivering through his muscles.

She barely knew him. Technically that was true. But she felt comfortable with him, somehow *right* in a way she'd never known before. It wasn't just a physical experience, either. She liked his long, thoughtful silences, his gentle teasing, his obvious love for the land that was so much a part of him. A wave of deep tenderness swept through her. No, it was more than *like;* it was love.

She should be thunderstruck. She should be denying it. She shouldn't be in love with a man she'd known for a week.

But she was. Deck completed her in a way she'd never known before. Instinctively she recognized the rightness of that completion, the forever quality to their coming together that would never be duplicated. And as she looked into the depths of his intense blue eyes, she nodded, giving him a trembling smile.

He lifted a hand and traced a finger around the outline of her lips. "Do you know how beautiful you are?" But he didn't wait for an answer. He lowered his head and sought her lips with his, and as he pulled her into the now-familiar whirlpool of sensual pleasure created by his touch, she found herself unable to summon the will to hold him off as she knew she probably should. As his lips firmed, demanded, entreated her to respond to his stirring kisses, she mentally shrugged her shoulders and gave herself to fate. How could this be wrong? With Deck, it would always be right.

His tongue danced over hers, then plunged deep in search of her sweetness and she wrapped her arms around his neck, holding him to her. She wanted to hold him forever.

She pressed closer, loving the solid strength of his big body, the tense clasp of his strong arms about her. The hand on her belly clenched spasmodically, then relaxed and she let out a little sigh of pleasure as he moved it slowly but steadily up to cover her breast. His palm was big and warm. Her flesh swelled and tightened beneath his touch and lightning-quick streaks of sexual pleasure shot from her nipple straight to her womb when he worried the tender peak between his thumb and forefinger. Her back arched, pushing her hard against him.

He responded to her unspoken cue, pulling his mouth away from hers to find its way down the column of her neck unerringly across the slope of her breast to the tip. When he closed his mouth over the fabric-covered nipple she nearly screamed aloud, squeezing her eyes tight shut.

He pulled back and her eyes flew open again.

"I want to see you." He dragged her into a sitting position before she fully comprehended his words. His hard hands streaked over her, tearing her shirt free of her jeans and roughly popping open buttons, burrowing beneath to the front clasp of her bra and snapping it loose. He smoothed the shirt back over her shoulders, taking the bra with it, and as his hand left small trails of burning sensation across her exposed flesh, she sucked in a breath. He paused, his eyes on the naked flesh he'd exposed and retraced his path, settling his palm squarely over the full mound. "Mmm, beautiful." His voice was a ragged murmur.

"This...is happening too fast." She was having trouble forming her thoughts.

His palm smoothed up her throat, then back down across the fine, soft skin to gently warm her other breast. "This is fate," he said quietly.

It was so close to what she'd been thinking that it startled her. Her gaze flew to his. His eyes were sober, a dark, unfathomable blue, boring into hers with a penetrating question she didn't understand, couldn't answer. "What?" she whispered.

Deck bent his head again, brushing tender kisses over her throat, down the midline of her body to the valley between her breasts. He turned his head and laid his cheek against her. "I have to do this," he informed her.

She knew what he meant. She felt it, too, this inexorable pull drawing her closer and closer, binding her to him. In answer, she slipped her hands up his forearms to caress his broad shoulders. He lifted his head and surveyed her with another of those unreadable glances, and as he did so, she stroked her palms across the solid muscles of his back, then drew them around to his chest, seeking the buttons down the front of his shirt.

As her fingers opened them one by one, steadily making their way down the fabric that lay between them, she heard his breathing change, felt him tense as her fingers burrowed beneath his undershirt and brushed over flesh. He took her hand in his and moved it up his body, flattening it over the heavy muscles of his chest. She felt the tiny point of his nipple beneath her palm as he slowly moved her hand in a small, steady circular motion which she quickly picked up and continued, even when his hand moved away and came back to explore the feminine bounty he'd uncovered.

Small flames licked at her self-control as she delicately stroked her hand across the soft fur that covered his chest, finding her way to his other budded nipple and rubbing her thumb across it. Her own breath was shallow and quick, streamers of excitement unfurling deep within her, creeping down to pluck insistently at her womb. Between her legs, a needy ache began. She felt herself soften and throb.

He suckled her, his hot mouth drawing her in, drawing at the stiffened peak until she began to whimper aloud at the overwhelming sensation his tongue produced as it curled around her sensitive flesh. Her hips began to shift back and forth as heated fireworks burst and embers shot down to further incite her body's gathering storm.

His hand had been cradling the plump pillow of her other breast, but he left it then, sliding down over the smooth, bare plane of her belly to the waistband of her jeans. She felt his fingers unbuckling her belt, deftly dealing with buttons and zippers, then the hot shock of his hard man's hand against her abdomen, sliding down to comb his fingers through the springy curls he found there. He toyed with her for a moment while his mouth continued to tease at her breast. But when she shoved her hips up at him, the motion caught his hand and she hissed in a startled breath as a hard finger slid between the soft, throbbing folds of her most secret flesh.

She was steamy with moisture and as he sank his finger steadily between her thighs, the slick dampness eased his passage and pleasured her as he stroked and probed, slipped and circled. Tension drew a coil of red-hot need tight, stretching and stretching until she ground her heels into the blanket on which he'd laid her, seeking relief from the taut, hungry torment. He found the pulsing bud that directed her body's response, and pressed with a gentle finger, and with no more warning than that, she exploded in his arms.

An avalanche of sensation crashed over her head, drowning her in its full fury. As her body heaved and thrashed against him, she was dimly aware of his deep whispers of encouragement, of his hand wringing every ounce of response from her until she lay limp and gasping for breath. She realized her eyes were tightly shut, and she opened them almost reluctantly, not wanting the sweet intimacy to end.

Deck was watching her intently, a half smile playing around her mouth. When she met his eyes, he dropped his head and pressed a kiss to her forehead, then sought her mouth. He kissed her deeply, possessively, and she was astonished to feel a distant throbbing in her abdomen heralding a return of the response she'd thought had to be exhausted.

Deck drew back and sat up. He came up onto his knees and shucked completely out of his shirt and undershirt. He was amazing, she thought with dreamy pleasure. His arms, chest, belly, everywhere she looked rippled with heavy, solid muscle from his daily work. No wonder his arms felt like steel beneath her hands.

He turned his attention back to her, stripping away her shoes and socks, shimmying her jeans down her legs and hooking his fingers beneath the tiny string-bikini panties she wore and tugging them off impatiently. He ran his hands over her with a rapt expression, as if he were memorizing her curves and textures, but finally he sat back with an impatient grimace and set his hands at the fastenings of his own belt and jeans.

He shoved them down in one rough movement, taking

his briefs along, and she was shocked by the full, obvious power of his body, cushioned in a thicket of curls several shades darker than that on his head. For the first time, she felt a quiver of nerves.

He leaned forward then, letting the weight of his body cover her as he took her face between his hands, his thumbs stroking her cheeks. "Don't be afraid." His voice was deep and hoarse. He kissed her, still lying full-length on her, and she realized with gratitude that he was giving her time to get accustomed to his body, to the feel of his hard power and strength. As her confidence returned, so did the lazy pleasure she'd felt and she let herself relax and enjoy the rising excitement his body inspired. A small hint of the tension that had drawn her before trickled through her and she shifted her hips back and forth, just enough to make him draw in a breath and lift his head to look down at her with narrowed eyes. "My turn," he informed her as he drew back.

He knelt between her legs and she glimpsed the small package he tore open. As he quickly covered himself, she watched with dreamy pleasure, another small pang of arousal penetrating her languor at the sight. Then he moved over her, drawing her thighs wider and settling his weight on her so that she could feel his hard strength snug between them, pulsing against her.

He reached for her hands, twining his fingers through hers and pinning both hands near her head. His blue gaze sharpened to the brilliance of a sapphire as he caught and held hers. Then, still maintaining the intense eye contact, he lifted his hips and she felt his solid length probing between her legs, pressing against the soft, throbbing portal. Her body opened easily, giving way to the steady pressure his hips exerted, admitting him in a hot, slick rush that made him grunt in surprised pleasure as he slid deep within her until he could go no farther.

She squirmed a little bit beneath him, loving the feel of him lodged deep but unaccustomed to the sweet invasion, and as she did, his fingers tightened almost painfully around hers.

"Don't." It was a harsh, whispered command.

She made a humming sound of arousal and amusement deep in her throat and wriggled her hips more purposefully as her confidence increased. "Why not?"

"Because." His breath caught on a groan and she surged upward against him, determined to break the control he seemed so reluctant to lose. "I want you too much. If I don't take this slow and easy I'm afraid I might hurt you."

She nearly smiled at that, but he was dead serious so she smothered it, contenting herself with another contraction of her hips that nearly dislodged him before ramming hard against him, driving him deep within her once more. "I won't break," she breathed.

He gritted his teeth. "Stop."

"No." She started to move again, and then the world became a wild blur of sensation and movement, a maelstrom in which she could do nothing but feel and respond. His fingers released her and burrowed beneath her to palm her bottom, tilting her up to better receive him. His hips surged forward and slammed into hers, then violently withdrew and surged again. He pounded against her with the inescapable force of a violent storm, her body quivering and shaking beneath the force of his attack until she felt herself explode again in his arms. As her body clenched in sweet spasms around him, he groaned and his body suddenly drew into a rigid arch, his hips pumping as his body finished his dance of passion, and finally they were both still but for their heaving gasps and the slowly diminishing pounding of hearts.

His breathing was still harsh in her ear, but he lay on her like a big, warm blanket. Around them, the sounds of the meadow began to return. She stroked her hands down over the slick, solid muscles in his back and he shivered involuntarily, then lifted his head to look down at her. "Are you all right?" he asked in a low voice, dropping a gentle kiss on her lips.

"I'm fantastic." She cupped his jaw in her hands, memorizing his features for a moment, then slipped them around his neck again.

His lips quirked, almost but not quite smiling. For long moments he continued to lie over her in a boneless contentment that she shared, but finally he lifted himself onto his arms and moved off her, easing out of her body onto his knees.

"Damn!"

She was startled out of her pleasant lassitude and she sat up hastily. "What's wrong?"

He was easing himself back into his briefs and jeans, and he reached to one side and snagged her clothes, handing them to her. "Our enthusiasm must have been too strenuous for my protection," he said, and there was an audible dismay in his voice. "It tore."

"Oh." She clutched her clothing to her while she considered. "It's probably not a problem," she said finally.

"Good." His whole body relaxed.

Why should she feel so hurt by his reaction? Nobody wanted an unplanned pregnancy, and she certainly was no exception. A baby with a man she barely knew would be a disaster.

But this is Deck.

That was it. She'd let herself acknowledge how much

she cared for him, and in some silly prehistoric corner of her femininity, a man who didn't want his woman barefoot and pregnant was rejecting her. And that really was silly, she chastised herself. It was the twenty-first century. No real man would do that to a woman. She should be glad Deck was concerned for her.

She shoved her arms and legs into her clothing and scrambled to her feet. But he caught her by the hand and pulled her into his arms before she could get on her shoes, dragging her against him and anchoring his hands in her hair. "This…meant a lot to me." He sought her mouth and as he kissed her, his tongue searching out hers and moving intimately into her depths, her heart grew light again.

She couldn't be wrong about the feelings growing between them. She sensed that he cared, just as she sensed he would need time before he could say it. And she had plenty of time to wait.

When they returned, he left her at her brother's house and took the horses back. In an hour he finished his evening chores, and after telling Marty he wouldn't be home for supper, he drove his truck straight to her place.

His mind was a whirling mass of confusion. Guilt and shame warred with satisfaction and deep contentment, anticipation alternated with self-doubt. Despite it all, when he stopped the truck before her house and saw her standing at the door, he knew there was no way in hell she was sleeping alone tonight.

"Did you have supper yet?" he asked her as he came up the walk.

Silver shook her head as she came out the door and perched on the porch railing, smiling at him. "I have a casserole in the oven. It'll be done in about forty minutes if you'd like to stay.''

Oh, yeah. He'd like to stay. Anticipation quickened his pulse, and his body stirred. He set his hands at her waist to draw her off the porch rail, but before he even realized he'd changed plans, he said, ''Put your legs around my waist.''

Silver's eyes widened. ''Why?'' Then comprehension dawned. Her eyes were a shining molten silver and her smile grew as she followed his command.

He held her in place with one arm while he opened the screen door and carried her inside. Though they both wore jeans, he could feel her sweet heat scorching him and his own ready desire brought him to a quick, full erection that walked a fine line between pleasure and pain where it strained against his pants. ''Because I want to drive myself crazy,'' he said sourly.

She laughed as he carried her through the house, then laid her head against his shoulder. The action warmed him in a way that had nothing to do with sexual fulfillment, but he shied away from thinking about how much he liked having her affection directed at him.

He mounted the steps to the second floor, then paused. ''Which room is yours?''

''First on the left.'' She pointed with one hand, then returned to the task she'd set herself, unbuttoning his shirt as far down as she could reach.

He muscled the door of her bedroom open and carried her inside, not bothering with a light. Late evening light brightened the big old bedroom well enough for him to see her, and that was all he cared about. Beside the bed, he let her slip to her feet, growling as his body reacted to the sweet pressure. Then he caught his breath as he felt her hands moving down his body. ''What are you doing?''

Her smile was pure anticipation as she worked at his belt and opened his pants. "Enjoying myself." Her hands slipped into his briefs and he couldn't breathe at all then, as her small, soft hands grasped him and pulled him free of his clothing. He clenched his fists at his sides while she explored him, his entire body focused on the sensations centered in his groin. She stroked up, then down, sandwiching him between her palms, wrapping her fingers tightly around him. The rhythmic motions pushed him perilously close to the limits of his control and in far too short a time he drew her hands away and lifted her to the bed, coming heavily down onto her. "What say we give this protection thing another trial?"

She smiled brilliantly as she lifted her hands to stroke his throat, his neck, his shoulders. "Okay. It really wouldn't be fair to draw conclusions after only one test."

"Clinical trials usually involve hundreds of samples."

Her eyes widened. "Oh! We'd better get started then."

And as he bent to kiss her laughing mouth, the hard shell in which his heart had been encased for so many years cracked open a little more.

Supper was nearly forgotten. Only the insistent, obnoxious buzzing of the oven timer that drifted up the stairs roused them from their absorption with each other's bodies.

After the meal, he helped her with the dishes and feeding the few animals on the property. The small domesticities felt comfortable, easy, with her at his side. He reminded himself for at least the twentieth time that he had an agenda here. But as he reached for her hand and strolled out of the barn, he faced the fact that he was going to have to make some adjustments to his original plan. When they reached the porch, he drew her down onto the front steps and settled himself a step above and behind her, wrapping his arms around her as she shivered in the cooling night air.

"Happy?" he whispered into her ear.

She nodded. "Yes."

They sat in silence then, watching the sun slowly tint the sky pink and orange in its dying moments.

Silver stirred, twisting herself around so that she could look up at his face. "That was beautiful."

"Umm-hmm." He inspected the upturned flawless features, then slowly lifted a hand and cradled her jaw while he lowered his head and took her lips. The kiss grew and heated between them. Her body pressed back against him and he groaned with pleasure at the feel of her sliding against his groin. It wasn't long before his pants were an uncomfortable prison and he slid his hands beneath her elbows, lifting her to her feet. "Let's go to bed."

She'd never slept with a man before.

It was a powerful, intimate experience, she decided when the alarm went off the next morning. Deck was possessive even in his sleep, cradling her against him with one strong arm throughout the night.

She caught her breath as she felt him stir against her, and he thrust an arm from beneath the sheets to silence the alarm. Then he turned back to her. "Good morning."

His voice was rough and early-morning gravelly, his jaw already stubbled with beard though he'd shaved before taking her to bed last night. Her heart swelled on a wave of love that nearly swamped her, and she had to close her eyes as she pressed a kiss to his chest. "Good morning."

"I've got cattle to move today." He rolled over, pinning her beneath him and she felt him full and ready, boldly pressed against her. "Tonight...I'd like you to come over for dinner."

"I'd like that." She lifted her hips the smallest increment, then dropped them again and felt his breathing catch.

"Stop that," he said. "I don't have time this morning." Then he dropped his head and kissed her thoroughly. "Better prepare yourself for my niece. She's a little out of control."

Out of control? She wondered exactly what he meant. While she was digesting that, he shoved aside the covers and slid out of the bed. He turned immediately and tucked the sheets back around her, then moved to the chair where most of his clothes had landed last night.

She rolled over onto her stomach and watched him dress, marveling at the hard muscle roping his body. He worked hard, and unlike the smooth muscles of the men at the gym she went to back home, his body showed the effects of his labors. He had a scar along one thigh, his tan was confined to his face, neck and arms, his hands were tough and calloused, and as he turned to snag his boots, she saw a large purpling bruise on his back that looked suspiciously like a hoofprint.

"Did you get kicked?" she asked, crossing her arms over a pillow and propping her chin on the back of her wrist.

He chuckled, twisting around to look in the mirror over her dresser at his damaged flesh. "Yeah. I'm breaking a three-year-old colt and he was being a smart aleck one day last week." He glanced over at her as he stomped into his boots. Then he crossed the room again, reaching down and hauling her into his arms. The sheet was wound around her, frustrating her efforts to put her arms around him, and he laughed as he bent his head and took her mouth. When he broke off the kiss, they were both breathing hard.

"I've got to get out of here or I won't go at all," he said, and there was a faint amused edge of desperation in his tone. "You're too tempting for your own good."

She smiled as he lay her back among the pillows. If she clung, pressed herself to him, she sensed he'd be crawling back into bed with her in a heartbeat. But something in his voice told her he wouldn't be entirely happy about it.

"I'll see you tonight," she said.

Twelve hours later, Deck cut the truck's engine in front of his house. "I guess I have to let go of you now."

Silver smiled, laying her head against his shoulder as he cuddled her closer with the arm he'd kept around her during the brief drive. "I guess you do."

Still, he made no move to get out of the truck. "I hope this wasn't a mistake," he said.

"What? Asking me to dinner?" She pulled away far enough to see his face. She wished she were sure enough of herself to know that wasn't what he'd meant, but the truth was she was frighteningly vulnerable and uncertain where he was concerned.

"Asking you to dinner wasn't a mistake." He dragged her back and kissed her before opening his door and preparing to unfold himself from behind the wheel. "Asking you to dinner *here* might put you off Strykers for life."

She laughed. "Your family can't be that bad."

He took her into the house through the kitchen door, and she saw a man and a little girl making salad at the counter. When the man looked up, she knew immediately that she'd have picked him out of a crowd as Deck's brother. Alike and yet…different.

Deck's brother, Marty, was a shade shorter and a shade more handsome. Or maybe he was just handsome in a different way, she decided, with hair the same chestnut as Deck's, his eyes a lighter blue and features that were classically beautiful without the brooding intensity of Deck's. His clothes were clean and pressed. Freshly shaven, he'd obviously just had a shower because there were still water droplets caught in the shining curls rioting around his head. If cowboys could make the cover of *GQ,* she thought, Marty Stryker would make the cut.

Still, her pulse didn't scramble and her palms didn't sweat when Marty smiled at her.

"Hi. You must be Silver. I'm Marty." He came around the counter to offer her his hand, flashing a warm, intimate smile at her that probably had legions of women fanning their overheated selves when he used it in public.

"Who else would she be?" Deck muttered from behind her.

Marty raised his eyebrows mildly, still holding her hand and gazing into her eyes. "If you decide you'd rather date the civilized brother, just let me know."

She laughed. "I'll keep it in mind."

"Da-*dee! Help me.*" The little girl still at the counter banged a wooden spoon imperiously on the edge of the ceramic bowl, causing Marty to wince.

"Easy, there, sugar," he said. He moved the bowl out of her reach. "Come meet Uncle Deck's friend."

"No. Don't want to." The child scowled at her father, then eyed Silver with the same baleful face.

Despite her ferocious expression, the little girl was beautiful, with long dark curls bouncing clear down to her waist and sky-blue eyes that were a carbon copy of her father's. As Marty lifted her down from the chair, she began shrieking, screaming a protest that would put a fire alarm to shame.

"This," he said through his teeth, "is Cheyenne. The joy of my life." He picked up the still-screaming tot under one arm and strode out of the room. "Back in a minute."

Silence descended as the noise moved farther and farther away.

Deck cleared his throat. "Marty'll put her in her room until she's ready to behave," he offered.

"She's so pretty," Silver said diplomatically.

"That she is. It's even easier to see when she's not throwing a fit." He chuckled. "Little brat."

"Will her mother be joining us?" She was almost sure of Deck's answer before he responded. The house lacked a feminine touch, though it was neat and clean and comfortable. She couldn't even say what was missing, but she was pretty sure Marty Stryker didn't have a wife hidden somewhere on the premises.

"No." Deck's voice held the echo of old pain. "She died when Cheyenne was two."

She was startled. She'd been expecting divorce, not death. "I'm sorry. That must have been terrible for Marty."

Deck nodded. "It's still no picnic."

"Raising children is difficult enough," she said, "without trying to do it alone. Marty's lucky he has you around."

"Oh, I don't know about that." Marty spoke as he reappeared. He calmly went back to finishing the salad, his big, rough hands competently slicing a tomato and radishes and sliding them into the bowl. "Most of the time it's like having a second kid around."

"Better be nice to me," Deck warned, "or I'll tell her about your ad."

Marty narrowed his eyes. ''How'd you like to fix your own meal?''

There was obvious affection between the two men despite their bantering squabbling. It reminded her of Cal, and she remembered that Marty also had grown up with her brother.

She smiled at Marty. ''My brother's not much of a cook, either. I think that's one reason he invited me out here.''

Marty turned away, picking up oven mitts and reaching into the top of the big double ovens on the wall for a tray of rolls that were finished browning. ''It was a surprise to have Cal show up in Kadoka again.''

''I'm sure. Have you had a chance to talk to my brother since he came back?''

There was a short silence.

''Uh, no,'' said Marty. ''I haven't.''

That wasn't a surprise, given the speed with which Cal had left town again after he'd arrived. ''He got called away for a few weeks,'' she told Marty. ''But I'm sure when he returns he'll be in touch. Deck tells me you and Cal are the same age.''

Marty nodded. ''Yeah. We got into plenty of trouble when we were kids.'' He glanced at Deck, and she followed his gaze, wondering at the almost hostile glare Deck was shooting at his brother. ''I'd better set the table. It'll soon be time to eat.''

He vanished into the dining room, leaving her to wonder at the tension in the air. Was Deck worried about her fancying his brother? The idea that he might be jealous was oddly pleasing.

A few minutes later, Marty called from the dining room, ''Meal's ready to serve.''

The conversation was light and easy during dinner.

Marty wasn't a fancy chef but the spaghetti sauce was tasty and he'd made brownies for dessert. As he set a plate of them on the table, his daughter silently appeared in the doorway.

Tear tracks stained her cheeks and her glossy hair was mussed. Her thumb was loosely tucked into her mouth as she eyed Silver.

"Hello, Cheyenne." Silver smiled at the little girl.

The child didn't answer, but her thumb came out of her mouth. Silver decided that was an encouraging sign. She patted the place setting beside her. "I bet you're hungry. I'd better hide a few of these brownies from your uncle Deck so you can have them when you're done with your spaghetti."

Cheyenne didn't smile, but Silver was pretty sure the air thawed a little. Best not to overwhelm her right off the bat, she decided, turning back to her own meal.

It was only a moment before the little girl scrambled up on the chair next to Silver.

"Would you like a roll?" She passed Cheyenne the basket, uncovering the warm, fragrant-smelling rolls as she did so. The child nodded and plucked a roll from the basket. While the men made coffee, cleared plates and clattered around in the kitchen, Silver matter-of-factly cut Cheyenne's spaghetti into manageable pieces and dished her out some salad. As she did so, she told Cheyenne she lived far away and began to talk to her about what it was like to live back East. By the time the little girl's plate was clean, she was chattering away, peppering Silver with questions and talking nonstop about familiar things around "her" ranch.

Marty cast her a grateful smile as he came out of the kitchen for the last time. "Hey, my midget," he said. "Guess what time it is?"

"Bath time!" This was clearly a favorite part of the child's day. She leaped out of her chair with a wild whoop of glee and raced back along the hallway, hollering, "See ya, Silver," as she vanished.

"You brush your teeth and get undressed. I'll be there in a minute," her father called after her.

Silver laughed in utter delight. "She's a charmer," she told Marty.

He chuckled. "Right. You don't have to lie. I know she's hell on wheels." His tone was affectionate but wry.

"She's lively and inquisitive," Silver protested. "There's nothing wrong with that. I think she's delightful."

"You wouldn't happen to have an identical twin stashed away somewhere, would you?" Marty asked. "That child needs a mother. Preferably one who can outsmart her. You were great with her."

As he rose and pulled out her chair, Deck snorted. "If you weighed a ton and had a face like a mad bull, he wouldn't want to know about your twin," he informed her. "Marty wants a wife more than he wants a mother for Cheyenne." He directed Silver into the living room and reached for her hand, drawing her down beside him on the couch.

"Not completely true, but I'll admit I'd like to get married again." Marty stretched his long legs and propped his boots on the hassock in front of his chair. "Nothing wrong with that."

"He's advertising for the perfect wife." Deck's tone was all informative innocence.

"Advertising where?" She had to concentrate on the conversation. Deck's thumb was rubbing small circles in her palm, and a tingling heat began to spread through her body at the familiar touch.

Marty cast his brother a ferocious frown that reminded Silver of his daughter's little face earlier in the evening. "Shut up, Deck."

But Deck ignored him. "In the personal ads."

That did get her attention. "In the personals? You mean the newspapers?"

Marty raised his eyes to the ceiling. "Why does everybody sound so shocked by the idea?"

"It just seems like a…a rather *im*personal way to find a spouse," she told him. She was doubtful and it probably showed. "Good luck."

"You sure you don't want to dump Deck and marry me?" His grin was pure devilment as Deck's blue gaze grew fierce.

"You ask her that one more time and you're going to be doing your wife hunting without a few of your teeth."

Marty laughed as he got to his feet and headed back the hall to bathe his daughter. "That's what I love about you, little brother. You're so predictable."

Silver laughed as Marty's voice died away, but the laughter faded to a whisper as Deck put an arm around her and drew her close. His eyes were blue steel and she searched his gaze without success. "What's wrong?"

He bent his head and set his lips on hers, pushing his tongue into her mouth and molding her body to his. When the kiss ended, she hung in his arms, breathless and bewildered. "You're mine," he growled against her lips. "My brother can find his own woman but he's not getting you."

"Of course he's not," she agreed, seconds before he took her mouth again.

They didn't stay long after that. In fact, she was almost embarrassed by the speed with which Deck hustled her out of the house and drove her back to her brother's place.

He didn't even ask if he could stay this time, simply took her hand and led her to the bedroom where she'd lain with him last night. His big hard hands streaked over her, baring her ivory flesh to his bold mouth and bolder touch and she gave him the total response that her heart demanded she share.

And if she was disappointed that he didn't speak of love or marriage or the permanence a part of her was longing for, she was sure it was simply that he wasn't quite ready for how fast their relationship was moving.

Six

The next evening Deck packed a light supper and two bedrolls and took Silver down to the southwestern end of the ranch, where the Badlands began in earnest. His grandparents and his parents each had lived in the little two-room cabin briefly after their marriage before they moved up to the big house.

He wasn't sure why, but he had a strong compulsion to show it to Silver. Not that it was any big deal. He reminded himself, for at least the twentieth time in the past few days, that this was a temporary relationship, begun for one specific purpose. The fact that her brother had gone away had given Deck extra hours to enjoy her before the inevitable day when he finally finished the business he had with Cal McCall.

And while he would regret it mightily if it affected his relationship with Silver, he still was resolved to do exactly that. But it didn't give him the pleasure it once would have. Instead of relishing the moment of reckoning, his mind shied away from imagining that confrontation. His dispute with her brother wouldn't affect Silver and him. He wouldn't let it.

His horse tossed his head, and Deck returned to the present in time to see a rattlesnake slither away through the rough rock. No sense in ruining the time he had left with Silver brooding about the future. He was going to take every minute he could get.

The ride down through the eroded buttes and gullies was beautiful in the late-day sun. In the places where the soft rock had already begun to wear away, thousands of years of history lay revealed in the striations of pink, orange, burnt umber, black and gray that characterized the Badlands. Their path took them south along the eastern edge of the rocks and then turned slightly east.

The land around the trail grew greener again, with cottonwood trees defining areas where there was water and hardy plum trees and aspens forming small stands of cover. He pointed out a wild turkey, a flock of sandhill cranes and an antelope that made a mad scramble for cover when it saw them coming.

In a little valley around the side of a hill stood the cabin, with the stable and shed ranged behind it like reinforcements. The land was green, and Indian paintbrush with striking scarlet tips grew along the small front porch of the cabin.

"This is beautiful," Silver said, and he could hear an almost reverent note of pleasure in her voice.

"My grandfather built it," he told her. "The bedrooms are the original sod house that he and my grandmother lived in when they first married. He built the front room and the porch later."

They dismounted and he showed her the inside of the

cabin. She exclaimed in delight over the small front room, with its rock fireplace dividing the kitchen from a living room area. He checked the bedroom for critters, then they swept out the main room and shook out the rag rugs that his grandmother had made. Silver insisted on doing a quick dust job while he built a fire. If they were staying longer than a night, he'd turn on the generator but there was no need. The fireplace would give them what light they needed tonight and they'd brought food.

Besides, he thought, grinning to himself, it wouldn't matter whether or not they had light for the activities he had in mind.

And it hadn't, he thought with satisfaction as they drove into town the following day. He glanced across the truck at Silver, noting the lavender shadows beneath her striking eyes. "We're going to have to start *sleeping* some of the time we're in bed."

Her face softened as she smiled at him, a warm, intimate expression that made his body stir restlessly in a response he'd have sworn he couldn't manage again right now. "Maybe we should sleep apart once in a while."

The suggestion was jarring. "That's the only option that's not an option," he said gruffly.

There was a small silence. Then Silver laid her palm on his thigh, squeezing lightly. "It was a joke," she said mildly. She stroked her palm gently up and down the length of his thigh in a reassuring touch. "Don't you know there's nowhere I'd rather sleep than in your arms?"

He felt better immediately. But his body was reacting with surprising vigor to her caress on his leg, and he took his arm from where he'd had it around her shoulder and clamped his hand over hers. "What I know," he said deliberately, "is that if you keep that up, I'm going to stop this truck right on the side of the road and show you what you're doing to me.''

Her eyes widened, and he caught her involuntary glance down at his lap. ''Amazing,'' she pronounced. ''Don't you ever get…tired?''

''Apparently not where you're concerned,'' he said wryly.

She laughed in delight. ''That's good.''

They were entering Kadoka, and as he turned right onto Maple Street he put both hands on the wheel. There would be enough gossip going around after people saw Silver and him come into town together without him fondling her in front of a crowd. He turned right on Main Street and headed for the elevator at the end of town, driving around a metal chair to which was taped a paper sign that reminded people of the rummage sale at the fire hall this weekend.

At the elevator, Silver stayed in the truck while he got out and went to find Sev. Stumpie was behind the cash register and Deck was inordinately grateful that the little man hadn't been in his usual post on the porch.

''Hey, Deck,'' the little man greeted him.

Deck nodded. ''Stump. Where's Sev?''

''Had to go over to the clinic. Etta Milsap's littlest boy cut hisself up purty bad foolin' around with his daddy's ax.''

Deck winced in sympathy. ''Bad business.'' He fished a list from his pocket and handed it to Stumpie. ''Here's some stuff my brother wants. You got it all?''

Stumpie glanced over the list and nodded. ''No problem.'' He slid off the stool and headed for the door. ''You back the truck around and we'll get her loaded.''

He went back out to the truck and moved it into position, but when he got back out, Silver opened her door and slid out before he realized what she was doing.

"Get back in. I'll be loaded in a minute," he told her.

But she smiled across the truck bed at him. "I'll help."

Stumpie heaved a sack of grain onto the truck bed with his one good arm just as Silver came around the end of the truck.

"Well, hello," he said, offering her his hand. "I'm Stumpie. You must be McCall's sister. Heard you was hanging around with this one, though nobody can figure out why."

Silver laughed, but Deck narrowed his eyes at the talkative little man. "It's nobody's business but ours."

Stumpie got the message. "Far be it from me to mess in your business," he said. He grinned at Silver. "Boy's a mite touchy today, ain't he?"

But Deck was too preoccupied to give Stumpie grief. It was the first time he, or anyone, had referred to Silver and him as a unit. Though the word *ours* had rolled easily off his tongue, the sound of it had hit him with the impact of a balled-up fist. It was a good feeling, one that warmed him in a way he never had felt before.

And he stomped on the little voice inside that reminded him he was merely using Silver because she could help him achieve a goal.

The dogs' barking dragged her from a sound sleep. She was warm and her head was pillowed on Deck's hard bicep. He slept beside her, apparently undisturbed.

A sense of wonder stole over her. Could this be for real?

Of course it could. Somehow a full nine days had slipped by since the first time Deck had made love to her beneath the pines. Since then they'd spent every moment together, when he wasn't working, and though she felt a little disoriented by the speed with which he'd moved himself into her life, it was a pleasant feeling. More and more, she caught herself looking into a rainbow-hued future in which she woke like this every day, in a home she and Deck had made together. They'd be busy with the ranch, but not too busy to add a child or two to fill their home.

The dogs were still barking, and their noise had taken on an edge of hysteria. Something was wrong. That wasn't just the stupid, ''there's-a-rabbit-in-my-yard'' bark. That was a for-real guard-dog sound. She sighed, knowing she'd better go see what the problem was.

She began to turn her head to check the clock beside the bed, but her hair was caught beneath Deck's body, and she squeaked when it painfully pulled at her scalp.

''Wha—'' Deck shot to his feet. ''What's wrong with those dogs?''

''I don't know.'' She chuckled. ''You always go from asleep to awake that way, don't you?''

In the moonlight, she saw him smile and shrug as he shoved a foot into his jeans. ''Yeah. I guess I do.'' He was still zipping his fly as he started for the door.

She'd been staring. She snatched up his shirt and followed him out the door, very aware that he hadn't bothered to put on underwear beneath the jeans. It was an erotic thought, and she had trouble focusing on the problem at hand.

At the bottom of the stairs, Deck cocked his head. ''I hear an engine.''

''An engine? Who in the world would be driving back our lane in the middle of the night?''

As one, they moved to the living room that stretched across half the front of the house and peered out the window. The vehicle crested the ridge and came around the corner, but it was too dark to see more than headlights.

"It's a truck," Deck said. He pulled her against him for a short but thorough kiss, then released her. "Once we get rid of whoever this is, we go back to bed." He glanced around. "Are your brother's guns in the study?"

She nodded, wondering how he knew Cal has asked her to place his gun rack in his study until she remembered the two men had been neighbors during their childhood. She supposed Cal's father also had kept his guns there.

"Stay here. Do not go outside until I get back." Deck hesitated until she nodded, then he turned and headed for the study.

Only a moment later he was back at her side, and she was shocked to see the rifle in his hand.

"Do you really think you need that?" she asked.

He shrugged. "Probably not, but why take chances? If this was someone coming with an emergency, they'd be blowing the horn and carrying on instead of just creeping along like that." He indicated the vehicle, which was just drawing to a stop.

"Oh." She peered through the curtains as a man got out of the truck. At least, she thought it was a man, as big as the person appeared. Then he walked under the floodlight on the way up the walk, and she gave a start. "Oh, my God. It's Cal."

"I thought he wasn't due home for another couple of days yet." Deck's voice was cold and flat.

"He wasn't." She was a little perturbed herself. Even if the two men had been childhood friends, this was going to be extremely awkward. "You can put the rifle back. I'll go out and talk to him."

Deck immediately disappeared. She watched as Cal

came up the path toward the house. Of all the nights in her entire life for a big brother to show up, this might be the worst. She twisted the knob of the front door and stepped onto the porch. "Hello. You're home early."

"Hey!" Cal gave her a hug as he stepped onto the porch. "Why are you up so late?"

"I was sleeping until the dogs started barking," she said, punching him playfully in the arm. "They scared me."

"Sorry." Cal looked over his shoulder at the two mutts, tails wagging eagerly at the foot of the steps. "I guess they haven't learned to recognize my truck yet."

"Either that or they're always going to greet you so enthusiastically." She cleared her throat. "I wasn't expecting you yet."

"Things wrapped up much faster than I'd expected. The guy panicked when the numbers didn't look right— it wasn't a big deal to get him straightened out." Cal gestured toward the gate. "Whose truck? Don't tell me you bought your own. I told you I had plenty of wheels around here."

She shook her head. "No, I didn't buy a truck." She hesitated. There was just no way to say it gracefully. "Cal...I, uh, I have company."

"Oh, okay. I thought you might get lonely out here." He hefted the briefcase in his left hand. "It's fine by me. They're welcome to stay as long as they like, if they can stand the remodeling mess. Friends from Virginia?"

"It's not a 'they.'" Silver twisted her fingers together and took a deep breath. "It's a 'he.'"

Cal had started to reach for the handle of the screen door. He froze. Slowly he turned and looked at her in the weak light, and she saw him eyeing the shirt that was all she wore…a shirt that clearly didn't belong to her. "A guy? Oh, hell. I really *am* sorry."

"Are you?"

She whirled, startled as much by the naked aggression in Deck's voice as by the way he'd silently come up to the door. Cal spun around as the screen door swung open. The man framed in the entry flipped on the porch light, and his beautiful features were stern in the harsh shadows from the overhead light.

"Welcome home, McCall." Deck gave his neighbor a slow, insolent stare. He was fully dressed except for his shirt, and she realized he'd gone back upstairs for his clothes while she'd gone out to talk to her brother.

Cal didn't say a word. But Silver sensed his sudden stillness as he took in the sight of the man.

"I guess you two already know each other." She stared hard at Deck, willing him to stop this…this whatever it was and be civil.

"Yeah." Cal's voice was expressionless. "We do."

"We do," Deck repeated.

"You son of a bitch!" Cal's briefcase hit the porch floor with a thud as he reached for the door. He yanked it open and grabbed a fistful of Deck's V-necked T-shirt.

As he drew back his fist, Silver launched herself at the two men, grabbing Cal's arm and hanging on with all her strength. "No! Cal, stop it!" She was screaming. "Just *stop it!* What's the matter with you?"

"What's the matter with me?" Her brother normally was one of the calmest people she'd ever met. Nothing seemed to get under his skin. She'd never seen him in anything approaching the rage that distorted his face now as she clutched his thick forearm, trying to stop him from pummeling Deck. "What's the matter with *me?* Did you sleep with him?"

"Did I—that's none of your business." She, too, normally was slow to temper but hers was boiling to a head.

"None of my business. Right." Cal shook his head like a bull enraged by a red scarf. He released his grip on Deck's shirt and spun to face her fully, shaking off her hand. "You mean it's a coincidence that my sister's been seduced by the man who believes I killed his sister?"

Killed his sister…killed his sister…killed his sister.

The words reverberated in her head and tore the air like roughly ripped sheets of paper, the ugly edges ragged and uneven.

She couldn't breathe, couldn't move. "What?" she whispered through frozen lips. "I don't believe it."

Cal took her by the shoulders and roughly turned her to face Deck. "Believe it," he said. "The only reason he romanced you is because he wanted to make me suffer." He directed his voice at Deck. "Isn't it?"

Deck was watching them with that same deep, unreadable look in his eyes that she'd seen before.

"Deck?" It was a hoarse appeal as she stretched out a hand to the man she loved.

He pivoted away from her.

It was only a movement, she told herself. So how could it have the power to break her heart in two?

She stuffed a fist against her mouth to stifle the agony that threatened to burst free. Cal put his hands on her again and drew her close, cradling her against his chest as if she were a small child.

"Get out of here," he said, his deep voice rumbling through her head where her ear was pressed to his chest. "You've done what you wanted to do. Now get off my land."

"Silver." It was Deck's voice from behind her. "Come with me. We have to talk."

She couldn't think, couldn't breathe. Burrowing deeper into her brother's protective embrace, she shut out the sound of the deep male voice.

"Get out." Cal's voice cracked like a whip. "She's done with you."

She didn't move during the tense silence that followed, nor when she heard booted footsteps receding. She still didn't move when a truck engine turned over and shifted into gear. It wasn't until the last sounds of the truck growling out over the ridge to the road disappeared that she let the tears come.

Cal supported her with one arm while he opened the door. He helped her into a chair and got her a drink, then perched his bulk on the edge of the long sofa. She took several deep breaths to stave off the hysteria that desperately wanted to break free, then raised her head and stared at her brother.

"Talk."

Cal spread his hands in an uncharacteristic gesture of helplessness. "Deck's family was my second family when I was growing up. His brother Marty and I were in the same class, Deck and his twin sister Genie two years behind us." He stopped, as if he'd run out of words.

"Why does he say you killed his sister?"

"I did, indirectly." Cal's face twisted in a spasm of grief and self-contempt as strong as it must have been years ago. "We'd all gone to a dance in town together. I got into a fight and screwed up my knee. Genie offered to drive me home. On the way—" He paused. "Silver, you don't know how sorry—"

"On the way what?" The last thing she wanted to do was dissect the thing that had just happened.

Cal sighed. "She was driving along bending my ear about some boy from Philip she was hoping would ask her out. It was dark, and there was no moon so it was hard to see. All of a sudden there was a big old steer in the road. We hit him broadside. My window was open and I got thrown out onto the road. Broke a couple of bones and banged my head. Genie—went through the windshield.''

Dear God. She wanted to comfort him. But even more, she wanted to *know.* ''Did she die right away?'' If they'd been traveling anywhere near the legal speed limit of seventy-five, she'd have had next to no chance.

''God, I wish she had.'' Cal rubbed his hand over his face, and there was raw agony in his voice. ''Deck and Marty came along as they were loading her into the ambulance. Deck went to the hospital with her. She lived less than a day.'' He raised his head and looked directly into her face. ''Deck said I killed her. If I hadn't gotten into that fight and needed a ride home…'' He shook his head, and she saw the despair in his features. ''He was right. I might not have been behind the wheel, but I am responsible for Genie's death.''

His face hardened into a mask of hatred. ''But that bastard had no business involving you—''

''I'm sure he doesn't see it that way.'' She was proud that her voice was so calm. ''He figures you hurt his sister, he hurt yours.''

''Yeah, but I didn't deliberately entice her into driving me home so I could get her killed on the way. He had a *choice,* dammit!'' He glared at her. ''Are you *defending* him?''

''No,'' she said quietly. Her breath hitched, and she stood abruptly, wanting, needing to be alone. ''There's no excuse for using me the way he did.''

Cal stepped toward her, but she waved him away. His

eyes were tortured, his face drawn as he watched her walk slowly to the steps and start up to her room.

But when she got there, the memories that slapped her in the face were too much. The pillows on her bed still bore the imprint of his head; the sheets, the scent of his body. As tears blinded her, she rushed forward and started stripping the sheets off the bed in a frenzy until she had no strength left, tearing the fabric free piece by piece and throwing it wildly at the wall where it hit with a flat, lifeless swish.

And then she slid to the floor and sobbed.

He caught a glimpse of her three days later.

Though he'd called the McCall house repeatedly, the machine had been the only answer he'd gotten. And no one had returned the messages he'd left, messages in which he'd begged Silver to return his call. He couldn't bring himself to explain through a machine the forces that had driven him.

Somehow, he *had* to talk to her.

Deck was inside the post office picking up the mail when he saw Cal's truck pull up in front of the vet's across the street. When Silver slipped out of the driver's seat to the ground, he quit breathing for a moment, until his burning lungs reminded him to take another breath. He stayed glued to the window, a futile, desperate longing grabbing at his throat.

She walked around the back of the truck, her long-limbed stride eating up the ground, and he couldn't stop watching the movement of her slender body beneath the new dark-blue jeans she wore. Less than two weeks ago he'd seen the full perfection of her body for the first time. Only three nights ago she'd lain in his arms and pressed herself to him; he'd touched her silky skin and buried his nose in the sweet-smelling hollow at the base of her throat and shared her intimate secrets.

It seemed like a lifetime.

She dropped the gate on the pickup, and he saw the old yellow dog lying on a blanket in the back. As she leaned in and lifted the dog to the ground, he clenched his fists against the urge to go over there and tell her she had no business lifting a dog that size.

She wasn't his to tell anything to anymore. For a few fleeting hours in the middle of the nights they'd shared, he'd felt happier than he had in years. And it was gone. By his own hand, he'd destroyed any chance he'd ever had with her.

As she vanished with the dog into the vet's office, he put a hand to the window glass as if to keep her from leaving.

"Deck Stryker! I'll skin you if you mark up that glass!"

Hastily, he removed his hand, scowling. Idell Samms had been the postmistress for at least the last hundred years, everyone swore. She was liable to come out and crack his knuckles with a ruler if he touched her precious glass again.

He looked across the street again, wishing Silver would come back out. He needed to talk to her, to see her face, to judge for himself how she was doing. Was she okay?

Okay? You're an idiot. Of course she's not okay.

How could she be, when he'd treated her so cruelly? As if what had passed between them meant nothing. But he'd been completely unprepared for Cal's intrusion into their idyll.

He'd been caught flat-footed. Half of him had silently gloated at the success of the vengeance he'd played out, however unwitting it had actually been. For years, *years,* he'd dreamed of making Cal pay. And he'd finally found his enemy's Achilles' heel.

The other half of him, the half that had a lock on his tongue while Cal hurled his fairly accurate accusations, had been appalled by the pain in Silver's eyes. He'd stood and watched her faith in him crumble and be swept away by the realization that she'd been nothing but a game piece in his strategy.

Only she was wrong. He'd watched her turn to her brother for comfort, seen the hatred that burned in Cal McCall's implacable gaze, and when she'd refused to listen, when she'd turned to her brother for the comfort *he* longed to give her, he'd been unable to find the words to explain. So he'd walked away.

He still couldn't explain it. How did he tell her he'd fully intended to use her from the first time he'd realized who she was? How did he tell her he'd sought her out with revenge in his heart? And how did he tell her revenge had tasted sour and crusty instead of sweet? That he still hated her brother's guts but he still wanted her so badly he ached at night? That he didn't know how he felt anymore but that he knew he'd done her a terrible wrong? That he'd do damn near anything if she'd come back to him?

He opened the door of the post office, crossed the wide main street, stopping for Sev's pickup loaded with feed bags and giving the other man a brief nod before going on to the vet's. He hesitated beside Cal's truck, but only for a moment. He had to see her.

Yanking open the door to the vet's office, he stepped inside. Every nerve in his body quivered. His gaze swept the room, but she wasn't anywhere in sight. She must be in the examining room with the doctor.

The receptionist looked up and smiled. "Hey, Deck. How's it going?"

"Fine, Amy Lee. You?" He meandered over to the shelves of medical supplies and pretended to look through them.

"Good," Amy Lee answered. She'd been a classmate of his mother's and she'd worked for Dr. Jim Karnes, the old vet, until his retirement. Now she worked for his son, Dr. Joe. "Can I help you find something?"

"No, no. I just need to pick up some Bangs vaccine." Which wasn't a lie. They *did* need to vaccinate the new calves. He perused the shelves some more, picking up stray items here and there, reading the labels and setting them down again.

"Silver Jenssen's in with the doctor," Amy Lee said brightly.

"Ummm." By now, thanks to Stumpie, he was sure half the damn town knew they'd been seen together. On second thought, half was probably a real modest estimate.

"She oughta be out any minute," Amy Lee offered.

This was ridiculous. He couldn't talk to Silver here. Abruptly he grabbed the vaccine and headed for Amy Lee. He fished money from his pocket, but as Amy Lee turned to hand him his change, the door of the exam room swung open and Silver stepped into the office area with the yellow dog.

She stopped dead when she saw him, and in her striking eyes the pupils flared. For an instant he read shock and panic and a deeply wounded spirit. Then a curtain of flat, blank indifference slammed down and he couldn't read anything in her expression. Her eyes flicked past him as she measured the room for a means of escape but he was standing between her and the exit door and after a moment she squared her shoulders in a tiny resolute gesture. The little motion bothered the hell out of him. Did she see him as some kind of monster to be faced down?

"Hello, Silver," he said quietly, ignoring Amy Lee's avid curiosity and the interested gaze of the vet.

"Deck." Her tone was neutral, her nod and expression reasonably pleasant. She turned back to Dr. Joe then, dismissing him as clearly as if he'd made a clumsy, unwanted pass.

"Thank you, Dr. Karnes."

The vet took the hand she held out. "It was a pleasure, believe me. The guy who used to own your brother's outfit didn't bring these dogs in for anything. When they got sick, he just shot them and replaced them. I'm glad you've taken an interest in this old guy."

"I suspect you'll see me again soon." Her voice was droll. "There are a couple of other needy souls hanging around the ranch."

"I'll just bet." The vet laughed as he disappeared again.

"Your brother's established an account, Silver," Amy Lee said. "Shall I just add this to it?"

She nodded. "Please. And thank you for everything. I'll give you a call when I get home, and we'll set up an appointment for the other dog and the cats."

Business concluded, Silver urged the dog toward the door. Realizing she intended to go around him without speaking, Deck reached for the door and held it open.

She murmured, "Thank you," without looking at him as she ducked past but he followed her right on out the door to her truck.

"You shouldn't be lifting him," he said as she put the tailgate down and prepared to lift the dog into the bed.

"He's too stiff to jump." She still didn't look at him, simply bent and put her hands beneath the dog's belly.

Deck bent, too, and gathered the dog easily into his arms, lifting him into the bed of the truck and ignoring the way she scrambled backward to avoid touching him. "There you go."

"Thank you." Her voice was as stiff as her features. She turned her back and slammed the tailgate shut, then walked toward the driver's door.

"Silver, wait." Hastily he caught up with her, stepping around her in time to open the door for her. "We need to talk."

She boosted herself into the driver's seat. This time she did meet his gaze when she spoke, and pain squeezed a tight fist in his chest at the tears shining in her unique eyes. "You're wrong. We needed to talk the day you decided to use me to make my brother pay for something he's agonized about his entire adult life. Now there's not a single thing we need to say."

Her lower lip trembled and she bit down fiercely on it. He reached out a hand, not knowing exactly what he intended but knowing she needed comfort as much as he needed to give it, but she yanked the door handle of the truck closed. He could have opened it again, could have dragged her out of her damn brother's damn truck right there on Main Street and proved to her that they could communicate just fine without words. But the searing agony in her silver eyes had branded itself indelibly in his head, stunning him into inaction.

It couldn't be too late. She had to let him explain, to…to fix it.

She gunned the truck's powerful engine then and backed out of the diagonal space without another glance at him. As he stared after the big truck, he was left with the image of her finely molded profile, marred by the bite she still had locked on the fullness of her lower lip.

A movement at the edge of his field of vision made him turn his head and look across the street. As he did so, the curtain over the window of the post office slipped back into place.

Great. If Amy Lee didn't broadcast the fact that Deck Stryker was making a fool of himself over Cal McCall's sister, Idell Samms would.

He didn't even care, as long as he got back in Silver's good graces. And her bed. He'd never met a woman who'd made him feel the way Silver made him feel. A woman who could make a man as happy as he'd been when he'd been with her had to be a good thing, and he intended to get her back no matter what.

Seven

She didn't go into Kadoka again for more than three weeks.

Cal made a trip in every other day or so to pick up mail, groceries, feed and other supplies they needed. She'd made appointments with the vet to have the rest of the animals that Cal had acquired checked and vaccinated, but he'd been the one to take them to town.

She made the drive to Rapid City several times to see Lyn and was encouraged by her physical progress, although the girl still seemed scared of her own shadow.

The first time she'd gone after Cal came home, Lyn had asked after Deck. It was almost too painful to discuss, but Silver forced herself to talk. She wanted to know everything she could learn about Cal's accident. After what Deck had done, she felt no compunction about pumping anyone who would talk about the sad memories.

"Deck won't be coming with me anymore," she'd said in response to Lyn's query.

Lyn's green eyes had filled with bewilderment. "Why not?"

"We're not, um, seeing each other anymore." Silver took a deep breath. "Turns out his interest in me was just a way to pay Cal back for Genie Stryker's death."

Lyn looked even more lost. "Why would he use *you?*"

She'd forgotten. With different last names, people didn't know she was Cal's sister. "Cal McCall is my brother." She watched Lyn's reaction carefully, clamping down hard on the lid of the raw pain that tried to escape its cage. Did everyone blame Cal for what had happened?

Lyn put a hand to her mouth to stifle an involuntary gasp. "He is? Poor Cal. I always felt so badly for him—" She stopped and Silver could see the light dawning. "My God. Everybody knows how Deck feels about that. You mean he…to get back at Cal?" Her expression was horrified.

Silver knew exactly what Lyn's small silence implied. She nodded, her throat clogged by the sympathetic warmth in the other girl's eyes.

"I'm so sorry." Lyn put her hand with its slowly healing bruises over Silver's.

"I'm not." She tried to make her voice matter-of-fact. "If Cal hadn't come home early, I'd still be believing that—that—"

"Snake?" Lyn suggested helpfully. "Yellow-bellied coyote?"

Silver had to smile despite her distress. "Pick one," she said. "They all fit." Then, to her complete and utter humiliation, she burst into tears. "I'm sorry," she said through the sobs she hastily tried to control. "It's just so…awful. I was falling in love and he was carrying out a plan. I'd like to kill him.''

Lyn nodded soberly. ''But are you sure that's all it was? He seemed so…''

''I'm sure.'' She shook her head firmly. No sense in harboring false hopes.

As she'd expected, Lyn was too reserved about her own life to pry more deeply into Silver's. She dutifully recalled everything she'd ever heard about the accident but there was no major information that Silver didn't already know.

In the weeks that followed, she kept to herself. She continued to work her way through Cal's house, painting and wallpapering places that probably had needed sprucing up when his father was alive. Cal solicited her advice on the two-story addition he wanted to put on, a combination mudroom, shower and laundry room that would keep the worst of the dirt out of the kitchen, which currently led directly to the side yard nearest the barns.

On the second floor, he planned to knock a wall out of the largest bedroom and create a master suite.

''That will still leave you with three big bedrooms up here,'' she pointed out. ''You're going to rattle around this place after I leave.''

He lifted his head from the plans he'd spread out on the kitchen table. ''What makes you think I'm going to be living here alone?''

She was flabbergasted. ''Is there someone you want me to meet?'' The thought was strangely unsettling. Stupid as it was, she'd never considered that Cal might get married in the foreseeable future.

He chuckled at her expression. ''I wish you could see your face!''

She stuck out her tongue at him.

He laughed again, then he sobered. ''That was just a

joke. There's no one special. But I plan to marry someday, so I might as well get this done now."

Marriage. The mere thought brought a resurgence of the heartache that was her daily companion. She'd been so stupid, weaving dreams about love and marriage with a man who probably still laughed at how easy she'd been.

"Sil?"

Cal's worried tone jarred her out of her misery.

"It's not too late to let me beat the living tar out of him," he said, a hard edge in his voice.

She knew who he was talking about, and she shook her head. "That would only add one more layer of angry feelings. That's the last thing any of us need."

"How about what *you* need?"

She shrugged. "I don't *need* anything." At least not anything she could have. "I'm thinking that after the party for Lyn next week I'll head home. By then I should be done with my interior decoration career."

"You know you're welcome to stay longer. In fact, I'd really like it if you'd stay."

But she shook her head. She could only take so many reminders of what might have been. Everywhere she looked, something else caught her eye and made her think of Deck. Talk of branding, a horse with white socks, tiny pines planted on a hill.... Every time she spotted a black hat her heart almost jumped out of her chest until she realized it wasn't him.

"No," she said. "I have to go home soon."

Cal didn't call her on the lie and she was grateful. He knew there was nothing drawing her home to Virginia. In fact, she'd complained about their mother's incessant matchmaking enough that he knew she was loath to return there at all.

"All right." His voice was gentle. "Whatever you decide is fine with me."

The little birthday celebration she was planning for Lyn gave her the excuse she needed to shop in "Rapid," as she'd heard the local folks call the city at the foot of the Black Hills. The next time she went, she drove up the hill to Rushmore Mall again and completed her purchases for the party, then took a deep breath and forced herself to walk into the large chain drugstore.

Bypassing the smiling face of the ice skater that endorsed many of the company's products, she walked to the section of the store reserved for personal feminine products. As she stood in front of the pregnancy-test kits, she realized her pulse was galloping like she'd just run a sprint.

Quit being silly, she told herself. *It's not the end of the world.*

She hadn't had a period in almost two months…and it had been six weeks since the first time she'd been stupid enough to sleep with Deck. It wasn't as if the results of this test were going to be any great shock. She knew she needed to go to a doctor, but she still couldn't bring herself to schedule an appointment. Then she'd have to face the fact that she was going to be an unwed mother, that she was going to have to break her parents' hearts and probably enrage her older brother beyond reason.

She forced herself to take the test the next day. And although she hadn't felt ill or unusual except for extreme tenderness in her breasts, she had a moment of light-headedness when she saw the color change on the little test strip, and she had to sit down on the commode seat lid until it passed. Quickly she bundled all the contents of the little box together and shoved it deep into the middle of the trash can. The last thing she wanted was for

Cal to find out right now. She was going to have to tell him eventually, but she had time for that.

The most urgent thing was seeing a doctor. Her hands shook as she called the first obstetrician she saw listed in the phone book and made an appointment for the following week, the day after Lyn's birthday.

When Marty called him to the phone saying it was a woman's voice, Deck moved faster than he had in weeks. *Silver!* was all he could think. The fact that there was no earthly reason for her to be calling him never even entered his head.

"Deck? This is Lyn. Lyn…Hamill." The soft, hesitant voice on the other end of the line was such a disappointment that he closed his eyes against the surge of feeling that swamped him.

"Hi, Lyn." It was an effort. "How are you getting along?"

"Fine. Uh…my birthday party is this Saturday. Five o'clock here at the house."

So why on God's green earth was she calling to tell him? "Um, that's right. I'd kind of forgotten." Lyn had gone to a woman's shelter not far from the hospital after her release, Silver had relayed the original invitation to the party he'd assumed they'd be going to together.

"Do you think you'll come?"

"Well…." He searched for an excuse.

She cleared her throat and said in a very small voice, "Silver will be there."

His entire body stiffened as the implications of the simple statement sank in, and he wanted to smack himself in the forehead. Of course she would. She was the one who had organized it in the first place…while she'd been with him. "Thanks, Lyn." His voice warmed. "I'll be there."

"Good." There was still a hesitant quality to her voice. "I hope I'm not making a mistake. She said you only—"

"*I* made the mistake," he interrupted. "And I want to fix it. I'll be there." As he hung up the phone, he blessed the kindness of Lyn Hamill's heart.

Silver would be there!

How could he have forgotten? He'd been trying to think of some way to get close to her for days. Weeks.

His first impulse had been to ride over to the McCall ranch and demand to talk to her, but he remembered the murderous look in her brother's eye. If he went over there, he and Cal were certain to get into a rip-roaring brawl, at the very least. And while he still would enjoy pounding McCall into a bloody pulp for what he'd done to Genie, he, Deck, wouldn't distress Silver any further for anything. The look in her eyes the day he'd tried to talk to her in Kadoka still haunted him.

He'd looked for her in town every time he'd gone in. In fact, Marty had started to look at him funny because he volunteered for every driving chore there was. But he was getting desperate. He'd seen Cal from a distance at least a dozen times. Once he'd been coming out of the insurance office when Deck was on his way to get feed and they'd stared each other down. They might still be there staring except Stumpie Mohler had driven up behind Deck in the middle of Main Street and laid on the horn to get him moving.

But there was no point in thinking about McCall now. All he cared about was Silver.

Maybe she'd forgive him if he apologized enough.

Maybe.

He'd been wrong to involve her in his desire to make McCall pay for what he'd done to Genie.

He didn't do anything and you know it. What about what you did?

The little voice that rose in his head was so unexpected he could only stand there and remember for a long, long minute. Then, snarling, he slammed it back into the dungeon where he kept it hidden.

Stomping out the back door, he went to get his toolbox. He had a tractor to fix.

On Saturday afternoon he told Marty where he was going. Then he showered and put on clean clothes, dusted off his hat and boots and took off for Rapid. The woman who ran the flower and gift shop on Maple Street had sold him a nice little basket he'd seen in the window. He'd had her fill it with candy and wrap it, and if he did say so himself, it was a pretty nice little birthday gift.

By the time he shut the door of the truck and walked to the women's shelter, a simple frame house, he was a nervous wreck.

A strange woman answered the door. She directed him through the hall to the kitchen, which led to a fenced yard.

There was a small crowd, maybe a dozen people altogether, gathered on the patio. Flower beds and planters had been filled with brilliantly colored annuals. Roses climbed the fence and perennials—some familiar wildflowers and others he didn't recognize—were worked into the landscaping around the edges of the yard.

Most of the people milling around were women. Most of them were probably…patients? Clients? Whatever they were called—who lived or had lived at the house. They were easily identifiable by the darting, slightly panicked looks they were giving him. For the first time he realized how intimidating a big man in a black hat might be. He couldn't do anything about his size but he could fix the hat, so he reached up and took it off, running a hand through his hair.

A woman with long, loose, red hair broke away from the group and came toward him, and he recognized Lyn.

"I'm so glad you came," she told him as she reached him.

Deck handed her the basket. "Happy birthday."

She stopped dead. Stopped talking. Her mouth hung slightly open, and she looked dazed. Almost as quickly, tears welled in her eyes. "Thank you so much," she said in her husky voice. "I've never—well, this is the nicest thing anybody's ever done for me. And presents…" She smiled, and a flash of wry humor flitted across her too-serious features. "Presents are the icing on the cake. No pun intended."

"Lyn!" A woman was calling from the long table set up on the patio. "You have to start the buffet line. You're the guest of honor."

Lyn looked around, then raised her hands helplessly. "I don't know the etiquette for parties," she informed him. Then, as she turned and started off, she glanced over her shoulder. "She's in the kitchen."

He didn't need to ask who "she" was. Though he hadn't seen her on his first pass through the house, he retraced his steps. Just as he reached the door, a woman backed through it carrying a large bowl of fruit salad. He recognized the wealth of black hair swirling around her shoulders instantly.

As she turned to start off into the yard, she nearly ran straight into him. "Oh! Excuse—*Deck!*" Her face paled, and he hastily grabbed for the bowl that threatened to slide out of her hands.

"Sorry," he said, assessing the color flooding back into her face. "I didn't mean to scare you."

"You didn't." She sounded annoyed.

"Ooo-kay." He wasn't going to argue. He indicated the fruit bowl he still held. "Want me to carry this to the table?"

"Yes, please." She started to follow him and he heard her say, "I didn't know you were invited."

"Lyn asked me to come." He set down the bowl in the space the women indicated and backed away. As he did, he snagged Silver's hand. "Come talk to me."

"No." She pulled her hand free before he could get a good grip. As she met his eyes and read his intentions, she said, "And don't you dare manhandle me in front of these women. They've seen enough abuse to last them a lifetime."

"I don't recall ever abusing you," he said, pitching his tone low. "In fact, I remember—"

"Stop it!" she hissed. "I told you before, there's nothing to say."

She turned and plunged back into the center of the activity before he could think up any good reason to keep her near him. All right. Fine. He could wait. But she *was* going to talk to him. Tonight.

The party was a subdued affair, but the warmth and affection the other women in the house showed Lyn told their own story. Only two other men were in attendance. One was the husband of a woman who volunteered at the home. When he'd retired, he informed Deck, his wife had found a whole new set of jobs to keep him busy. Now he did routine maintenance at the home.

The other man was a local landscaper who donated his time to teach the women how to care for the plants and gardens. Both men made a beeline for him and he wondered if they were as relieved as he was to find someone else who could talk about the Twins' chances of winning the pennant this season.

Finally the last gift had been opened and the cake was a sloppy pile of crumbs. The women had the place cleaned up faster than he could offer to help, which suited him just fine. And just about that time he realized Silver had disappeared.

Saying a hasty goodbye to Lyn and his new buddies, he made it to the front door just as her truck pulled away from the curb.

Traffic in Rapid wasn't usually much to speak of, so he took his time getting his own truck moving after her. She probably thought she'd made her getaway—

He was so busy congratulating himself he nearly missed her signal and subsequent turn into the lot of a small motel. What the heck was she doing?

He didn't think she realized that he'd followed her until he pulled his truck into the parking lot. She was already out of her car. Was she visiting someone?

When she turned and saw him walking toward her, her whole body almost seemed to sag. Ignoring him, she started to walk across the macadam.

His legs were a whole lot longer than hers, and unless she actually ran from him, she couldn't hope to outdistance him. He reached her side in a matter of seconds and as he did so, she halted.

"What do you want?" Her face was as mild as her tone, but he noted the way her fingers clutched the strap of her bag. She wasn't as calm as she wanted him to think.

You. "I told you before. I want to talk to you."

"Look," she said with a hint of impatience and perhaps the smallest dash of belligerence. "I'm tired. As *I* told *you* before, there's nothing to talk about."

He ignored that. "Ride home with me. After we talk, you can sleep the rest of the way."

"I'm not going home. I have a room here for the night because I wasn't sure how long I'd be and I didn't want to drive back alone late at night."

I could have brought you, and then you wouldn't have been alone. But he didn't say the words. Instead he reached for the key she took from her purse. "Which room is yours?"

"Nineteen," she said through what sounded like gritted teeth. "But you are *not* invited in."

He ignored that, too, walking the rest of the way to Room Nineteen. He unlocked the door and stood back, motioning her to precede him. She hesitated, but she finally stepped into the room. When she did, he followed her so closely there was no way she could have slammed the door in his face.

Silver immediately made for the far side of the room. He shut the door and turned the dead bolt. "Sit down."

"I don't want—"

"Sit down."

She sat.

She chose one of the two chairs at the tiny table beneath the window at the back of the room. Folding her hands atop the table, she placed both feet on the floor in the guise of an attentive student.

"Thank you." He felt stupid. "All I want is one chance to explain."

She didn't say a word.

He sighed. He walked across the room and eyed the fragile chair, then sat on the edge of the bed. "I'm sorry. I should have told you."

She was looking at the table, not at him, but he saw her bite her lip.

"I guess it's hard for you to understand." He hesitated. He *hated*, positively hated, to even think about the accident, much less talk about it, but if he wanted Silver back he'd have to do it. "Genie was my twin," he said. "We shared everything it was possible to share. We even had our own language when we were toddlers. It drove my parents and Marty crazy, so they say. When she was— when she died, I felt like part of me had died, too." He put a hand to his chest. "Something in here just shriveled up and it hasn't been the same since."

She looked at him then, and there was compassion in her eyes. But he wasn't finished.

"I've carried a lot of anger around for years. When I first met you, I thought you were the most beautiful thing I'd ever seen. Then I saw you get into McCall's truck and I figured you came to town with him and I hated him even more. Then…" He didn't like to think about what he'd done. "I found out you were his sister. I intended to stay away from you. I didn't plan it, I swear. At least not at first."

The warmth had cooled in her steady gaze, though she was still looking at him. "Well, that's something," she said in an expressionless tone.

"Genie was special," he said. "She would have been the life of that party today—" He stopped, as his own words penetrated his mind.

Guilt hit him with the force of a blizzard howling across the unprotected plains. *Genie. Party.* He'd been so wrapped up in thoughts of Silver that the month had gone almost by and he had barely thought about his sister. Her birthday—and also his own—was coming up a week from today. If she'd lived, they would be turning thirty together.

God, how could he have forgotten her?

"Deck?" Silver leaned forward slightly.

He shook his head, holding up a hand. Then he abandoned the effort and raised both hands to his face, bending nearly double beneath the weight of his pain. He tried to imagine what she would look like now, at thirty, but he had trouble even calling up the image of the sister he'd loved all those years ago.

How could he have forgotten her?

The mattress tilted slightly as Silver sat beside him, and he felt the warmth of her body next to his, her arms circling his shoulders. Her hair whispered as she pulled his head to hers, and she held him while the pain battered his senses and beat his emotions raw again.

He sat in the quiet room with a woman's warmth surrounding him, and he grieved as he hadn't since the day he'd stood by while they lowered his sister's casket into the ground. He'd placed the bridle from her little mare on the casket and clenched his fingers around the class ring he'd carried in his pocket—the ring that was a twin to his.

And when the funeral ended, the great gaping hole in his life had been raggedly pulled together, but a pocket of unhealed emotion remained, festering for years until the day Cal McCall came back to town.

The room grew quiet around them. He realized that Silver was rocking slightly, comforting him with wordless noises that soothed the hurt in his heart. He straightened and put his arms loosely around her, his face still close to hers. "Thank you," he whispered.

"You're welcome." She whispered, too, and her breath was sweet on his face. It seemed the most natural thing in the world to turn his head and find her lips with his own.

Her mouth was soft and sweet under his, and he drew

her closer, loving the familiar feel of her, relief flowing through him. He'd been afraid, deep down, that he wasn't going to be able to make her believe him, to make her see that he hadn't just been following a plan by the time they'd made love, that he'd fallen in love with her. *He'd fallen in love with her. He loved her.* He'd felt it, but he hadn't acknowledged it until now.

But he was going to have a chance to show her what she meant to him. She still loved, him and everything was going to be all right.

She was a fool and she knew it.

But as Deck's mouth took hers and his tongue slipped slowly around the outline of her lips before gently moving on, she knew she was going to take this night as one last gift from the gods. Despite everything that had happened, she loved this man. And because she did, she couldn't resist him when he needed her.

He needed her now, she was quite sure. He'd needed comfort of a different kind earlier, and she'd been able to give him that. Now she could offer physical ease, and as his hands moved over her, she was glad that he needed her this way. He might not love her but he *needed* her.

And when she'd gone, he would remember this. Remember that she'd been kind and caring and…and loving, when she could have turned him away.

Their mouths clung as he urged her to her feet, then stripped back the sheets on the bed and drew her down. Slowly he removed her clothing and let her help him with his until there were no barriers and they were hot, hard skin to soft, sleek skin; strong, steely man to yielding, wanting woman.

When he kissed his way down the slope of her breast and took the taut peak into his mouth, she couldn't catch back the wince that escaped. The reason for her ultrasensitivity fluttered on the tip of her tongue but she swallowed the words that wanted to blurt themselves out. Her baby wasn't going to become anyone else's problem. "Be gentle," she breathed.

"I'm sorry." He immediately softened his fierce assault on her sensitive flesh, and she made a satisfied noise of pleasure at the sensation that streaked through her. He remembered everything, how she liked to be touched, where his callused fingers elicited the strongest reaction, what his questing mouth and hands could do to bring her to a writhing, moaning peak. But too soon, he moved over her and parted her legs.

Then he paused. "Wait. I have to—"

"No." She caught at his shoulders. "You don't have to."

He hesitated. "Are you sure?"

She laughed, hoping he didn't question the source of her amusement. "Positive."

He didn't question her again, simply put his hand between them and eased himself into her. He filled her so completely, so gently and sweetly that she felt tears come to her eyes. If only—

"Am I hurting you?" His voice was deep and hushed. *You're breaking my heart.* "No."

He made a skeptical sound, lowering his head, and she realized he was licking away the tears that had slipped back from her eyes into her hair. "Silver, I—"

"Shhh." She put a hand over his lips, muffling the sound, then slipped her hand aside and replaced it with her lips, kissing him so fervently that he followed her lead, and she knew he would forget about talking.

Her body was hot, slippery, silky, the feel of his naked flesh a powerfully seductive sensation. Her hands streaked over him like lightning as he immediately began a steady motion that pleasured her with every stroke. She was panting beneath him, damp hands stroking over his body. Palming his buttocks, she pulled him hard against her, and he took her hips in his big hands, angling her up so that his thrusts crashed against her pelvis in a frantic rhythm that she welcomed. After only a few moments he began to surge against her. The world receded as she clung to him, accepting his domination until, with a small whimper, she began to convulse beneath him. Her back arched, her legs climbed his back and her inner muscles caressed him in tight, steady waves. Within seconds he climaxed, emptying the pulsing jets of his seed into her until the full weight of his big, utterly relaxed body pressed her into the mattress.

Long moments passed, moments in which her thundering heartbeat slowed and settled into a steadier rhythm. Deck's breathing became less tortured, his body even more boneless. At one point he lifted his head from where it lay beside her ear and muttered, "Am I getting too heavy?"

"No." She whispered the word, tightening her arms around his neck.

They lay in silence for a long time. Finally Deck rolled over, keeping his arms wrapped around her so that she simply switched places with him.

"I want to tell you again that I'm sorry."

Her head lay on his chest; she didn't lift it. "Thank you."

That apparently satisfied him. "I'm sorry that I didn't—"

"Not now." She still refused to lift her head from his chest. She could hear the strong beat of his life force in his heart's repetitive rhythm, and she focused on that to ease the sadness creeping into her mood. She was going to remember every moment of this last time, imprint it in her mind to warm her on the cold, lonely days she knew lay ahead.

"All right." His voice was tender, and his big hands stroked up and down her spine, slipping over her so gently she wanted to cry again. "I don't blame you for still being mad. It'll take time for you to forgive me. I can live with that."

But I can't.

She didn't say the words. He would never accept her saying them, because he was determined to have her. But he didn't love her. She knew that. She'd been a means to an end, and he'd decided to enjoy her for a while. He'd never said anything about permanence. He'd said she was beautiful and that he'd wanted her. And clearly that hadn't changed.

But all that was beside the point. She stroked her hand over his chest in sad acceptance. He'd used her and no matter how much she might care for him, she would never trust him again. He wasn't after her money. But he'd used her in another way, a way that made marrying a woman for her fortune seem almost benign in comparison.

Deck had used her to hurt her brother. And she couldn't, *wouldn't* ever let him do it again.

Eight

He damn near *danced* through his work the next morning, even though he had gotten home barely in time to get himself redressed to start another day. Okay, so maybe Silver had been reserved and quiet except for the times during the night when they'd made love, but he expected that. Everybody knew women liked to hold things over a man's head for a while.

Once she'd gotten that out of her system, he would figure out where to go from here. He wasn't exactly sure what was going to happen. He hated to force her to choose, but he didn't plan to let her get away from him again. And that meant defying her brother. It was going to hurt her, no matter how supportive he was. But they'd get past it. He would make sure of it.

Marty came out of the barn on his bay gelding mid-morning while Deck was repairing the fence around what passed for Marty's vegetable garden. Deck tried to wipe the silly grin off his face, but his brother slowed and stopped, eyeing him as if he'd sprouted horns.

"What's up with you?"

"Me? Nothing."

Marty snorted. "At breakfast, you were whistling. You *never* whistle at breakfast. A grunt is usually the limit of your conversational appeal. Now you're walking around here smiling like you just won the lottery."

"Maybe I did."

"Maybe that lottery is why you didn't get home until six o'clock this morning."

"Maybe."

"You went to Lyn Hamill's birthday party yesterday. Would there have been a certain silver-eyed fox at the same party?"

"Maybe."

"Does this mean she's off-limits again?"

Deck felt his good humor slip a notch. "Definitely."

"Hmm." Marty raised his eyebrows. "Not *maybe?*"

"Definitely not *maybe.*"

"I see. So where does the fact that she's McCall's sister enter into your delirium?"

Deck scowled. "Hell if I know." He stood and stretched his limbs, and his voice was sure and hard when he spoke again. "All I know is I still want her and I've still got her. And I intend to keep her, no matter what her damned brother says."

Marty nodded. "Whatever you say." He hitched his thumb in a generally southern direction. "I'm going to ride down toward the river bottom today and see if those buffalo have come through the fence anywhere. If I'm not back by dinner, how 'bout I meet you at the city bar later?"

Deck nodded. He knew his niece, Cheyenne, had spent

the night with her cousins, and Marty had probably talked his sister-in-law into keeping her a second night. "Sounds good. If my plans change, I'll leave a message there." Then he remembered the ad Marty had shown him weeks ago. He'd been so wrapped up in his own problems he hadn't given it a thought, but now he was intensely curious. "You have any takers for the position you advertised?"

Marty narrowed his eyes. "I might have."

"I'll be damned." For the first time in days he laughed aloud. "You did! Who is she?"

"I've had two answers so far." His brother's voice discouraged questions.

It had no effect on Deck. "So did you meet them yet?"

Marty nodded. "Yes. Neither one of them was quite what I had in mind."

"You mean neither one was a beauty queen?" Everyone around knew Marty had always had an eye for the prettiest girls. His wife had been the homecoming queen and just about the most beautiful girl in Jackson County.

"They were both very nice."

"But...?"

"But nothing, you Nosey Parker."

Deck pulled his face into serious lines. "Wow. You must have struck out big-time if you couldn't convince either one of them to marry you."

"I did not 'strike out,'" said Marty. His voice was aggrieved. "You want to know all the dirty details? Fine, here they are. The first lady advertised her age as mid-thirties, but when we met it was pretty clear she'd had a memory lapse because she was fifty if she was a day. The second one...well, let's just say the second one thought drinking one beer meant I was an alcoholic. She also was appalled that I don't take Cheyenne to church on a regular

basis and gave me a two-hour lecture on the evils of the
world.'' He shook his head, smiling at his own predica-
ment. ''Needless to say, I didn't call her again.''

Deck crossed his arms. ''I told you this was a stupid
idea.''

''It's not a stupid idea. I just have to keep trying.''
Marty turned his horse and began to ride away. ''When I
find the right one, I won't have any trouble convincing
her I'm a great catch.'' He grinned as he looked over his
shoulder at Deck. ''Unlike some people I could name.''

Marty was late getting to the bar in the evening.

Deck wasn't in the greatest of moods to start with.
Marty's comment had been a joke, he knew, but it had
stuck in his craw. Then he'd called Silver half a dozen
times during the day, but there was no answer at the
McCall ranch. He didn't want to leave a message in case
her brother hassled her about him. Dammit! After last
night he'd expected she'd be waiting to hear from him.

Maybe she was. Maybe Cal had been around and she
hadn't wanted to answer the phone with him hanging over
her shoulder.

His mood grew darker while he ordered a pizza and ate
the whole thing himself. This situation wasn't going to
last for long. Silver was going to have to tell her brother
to back off and let her—let her what?

Date him? The relationship in his head didn't feel much
like something as casual as dating. He knew she loved
him. At least, he was pretty sure she did, and he loved
her. But where did they go from there? He couldn't imagine making her choose between him and her brother.

He was standing on the edge of a steep plateau in a
high wind, staring down into a place he'd never imagined
himself going. Problem was, it was like the middle of a

moonless night and he couldn't see *where* he was going. Or where this relationship was going. He couldn't see a future that ended with everyone happy, and he didn't much like the fact that it scared the hell out of him.

The door of the bar opened and he glanced at the new-comers just like every other person in the place. Marty came in, spotting him and heading toward his stool at the bar. Then the action in the room seemed to slow and stop as the door opened again and Cal McCall stepped in.

In an instant, all earlier thoughts were wiped away. The familiar burning fire in his gut flared as his former friend let the glass door slowly shut behind him.

McCall's face was frozen into a rictus of rage, his gaze fierce as he scanned the room. In less than a second, the eyes that were a darker version of Silver's zeroed in on him, and Cal strode across the floor.

"You lousy bastard," he said to Deck. "Get up so I can knock you down."

"My pleasure."

Despite Marty's harsh protest and the aghast murmurs behind him, Deck slid off his stool and spread his arms wide, eyeing the man whom he held responsible for his sister's death.

The space between the two men narrowed and hardened into a sheet of thick, freezing ice. Deck stared at the familiar gray eyes, unblinking, as a parade of years galloped through his mind: wild races on horseback, swimming in the river, speculating about which girls would do it and what a virgin would be like, lying through their teeth about what they'd done with whom last Saturday night...but always ending, *always,* with the moment that had changed all their lives forever.

The big man bared his teeth. "I should have killed you when I caught you with my sister."

Deck smiled, but it wasn't a friendly expression. "You and what army? You want to talk about sisters? We can talk about sisters any day of the week. Tell me, McCall, have you done anybody else in since you killed *my* sister?"

Behind the bar Lula May gasped, and the sound hung in the still, smoky air. Slowly McCall flexed his hand. His lean features hardened into a black mask of anger that would have made a lesser man shrink back. "I didn't kill your sister," he said through his teeth. "God knows I'd have traded places with her if I could have, if only to spare the *decent* members of your family their pain."

"Huh." Deck loaded the single syllable with contempt.

Marty stepped forward. "Let's take this outside," he suggested in a low voice.

"Why?" Cal never looked away from Deck. "So nobody will hear what *he* did to *my* sister?"

"I didn't do a damn thing to your sister that she didn't want me to do." Deck was goading the bigger man, and a perverse part of him was enjoying every minute of it. He saw Cal's shoulders tense and his weight shift from foot to foot and he knew McCall was about to take a swing at him.

Good. If Cal wanted to beat him to a pulp he wasn't going to stop him. *Because he was as much at fault for what had happened thirteen years ago as Cal had been.*

It had been years before he could let himself admit it, years before he could face the fact that Cal wasn't the only one who'd made a mistake that night. He, Deck, wasn't blameless in Genie's death. Cal had come to him first for a ride home. He'd been all too happy to dump Cal on Genie when she'd offered to take him home, all too happy to wash his hands of anything that might interfere with his overactive teenage libido. He'd been treat-

ing Cal McCall like road dirt for years in his dreams of
revenge, forgetting—or refusing to face that fact—that
he'd been just as thoughtless as Cal that night.

*And the way you treated Silver isn't going to win you
any medals, either.* Somehow, letting the other man beat
him senseless seemed like a fitting punishment. He forced
himself to smile through the pain that lanced through him.
"As I recall, Silver liked what I did so much that she
begged me—"

He never finished the sentence. Cal's immense fist
came flying at him, catching him solidly on the jaw and
knocking him back across a table. *I will not fight back.*
Despite the rage coursing through him, he repeated the
sentence over and over.

As he struggled to his feet, Cal came to stand over him.
"That's for making my sister cry. This—" He hammered
Deck again "—is for getting her pregnant and walking
away from your responsibility."

Stars were exploding in his head. He was dimly aware
of the shocked reactions of the other patrons in the bar to
Cal's words, but the shock wave rolling through his own
system nearly obliterated anything else.

Silver was pregnant?

Lula May was trying to get him to sit down and put
ice on his jaw, but he struggled to his feet again while
Marty and two other cowboys were restraining Cal. "I
never walked…" Cal's words were reverberating in his
head with the steady force of a jackhammer. "Silver's not
pregnant," he said. "She can't be."

Ha. Remember the first time…?

"Oh, no?" The other men had released Cal, and the
rage crackling from him seemed to have evaporated with
the second blow. He hung his head as if he were too
weary to hold it up. "I found directions for a pregnancy

test kit on the bathroom floor today, and when I confronted her, she told me herself. So don't tell me she can't be. You self-centered, worthless cowboy. Do you think you're the only person in the world who misses Genie?''

He jerked a thumb over his shoulder at Marty. "What about her *other* brother? What about her friends? Have you ever really *thought* about how I feel? At least you don't have to live with the knowledge that your behavior cost her her life.''

Oh, but I do. You aren't the only one with blood on his hands.

Unaware of Deck's tortured thoughts, Cal's lip curled as he stared at Deck with naked hatred on his face. "I'm only giving you one warning. If you come near Silver again, I'll kill you.''

As Cal turned and slammed out of the city bar, Deck stood blankly, his mind so focused on Cal's words that little else penetrated his brain. *Silver was pregnant.*

Then he realized Marty had a hand under his elbow. "Let's go home.''

Irritably, he shook him off. "Let go. I can walk.''

"Fine.'' Marty held up both hands. "Come on.''

They'd each driven into town, and they each drove home. When they got back to the ranch, Deck climbed out and walked to the porch steps, where he cautiously parked his butt on the top step. His jaw was aching and he hoped that damned McCall hadn't broken it.

But the thought held little rancor. For years he'd nursed his anger against Cal, and now, in the space of one evening, it was all gone. He felt numb. And not just because of the fight.

Silver was pregnant.

And he knew exactly when it had happened, too. That first time, the only time their protection had failed.

God, he *had* to talk to her! Though the impulse to go to her immediately was strong, he forced himself to wait. Another confrontation with Cal would only distress her more, and that was the last thing he wanted to do. Tomorrow he'd ride over to McCalls'. As soon as Cal was gone for the day he'd go into the house, make her listen to him.

Marty sank to the step beside him and stretched his legs out. "I know how you feel about this whole mess," he said quietly. "Genie was my sister, too."

"You're wrong." Deck turned his head and let his brother see the shame he'd hidden for so long. "You don't know how I feel. Cal came to me first for a ride home. If I'd left with him, maybe things would have turned out differently."

"Like how?" Marty's voice was sharp. "Like maybe you'd be dead instead of Genie? She was *ready to leave,* as I remember. If you'd gone with them, I might have lost both of you." His voice cracked. "Sometimes I feel like only half of you was left after she died, anyway. You two always did have a special relationship that left the rest of the world out in the cold."

The misery in his brother's voice grabbed at Deck's conscience. "I never meant to make you feel—"

"Well, you did." Marty stood, looking out into the darkness that surrounded them. "I'm sorry Genie died. I'd have taken her place if I could have. But I can't, and neither can you." He nudged Deck gently with the toe of his boot. "We still have each other. And Cheyenne. And it sounds like you've got a shot at a whole lot more than that, if you don't blow it."

"I have to see her." He said it quietly.

"You'd better be darn careful." He noticed Marty didn't bother telling him not to go near Silver. He knew better. "Cal's pretty pissed. And with good reason. You jerk." But his tone was fond. "What are you going to do now?"

Deck heaved himself to his feet and followed his brother into the house. "Marry her."

He rode across the acres that separated the two outfits the next day at dawn. Settling himself in a copse of trees on a ridge downwind from the house, he pulled out the binoculars he'd brought along and prepared to wait. The minute Cal was out of there, he was going to talk to Silver.

But as he sat there, letting his horse graze idly, something niggled at the back of his mind....

No.

Now that he was finally where he thought he'd wanted to be, it felt wrong. After a long moment of indecision, he raised the binoculars. He still was prepared to wait, but with a different goal in mind. There was something he had to do before he talked to Silver.

Around nine, he saw Cal come out of the house and get into his shiny new truck. Instantly, he wheeled the gelding and started for the lane that ran from McCall land to the highway. The lane meandered through the countryside in a way that gave him an easy ride, and when Cal crested one hill about halfway out to the road, Deck had reined in the horse and was waiting for him.

He could tell the moment Cal spotted him. The truck slowed to a less-than-gentle halt. Cal swung out of it seconds after the engine died and started to walk toward him, and his eyes were as flat and cold as a winter storm sky. "I told you what would happen if you came near my sister again, Stryker."

Deck dismounted. "I'm not here to talk to Silver right now."

Surprise slowed Cal's charge. "No?"

"I'd like to talk to you, if you'll give me a minute before you end my life."

Cal's eyes flickered. Deck wasn't sure if it was rage or amusement, and when the bigger man's set shoulders relaxed, a ripple of relief ran through him, though he was careful not to show it. He could hold his own in a fight anyday, but he'd promised himself he wouldn't hurt Silver's brother no matter what. He hadn't been looking forward to getting slammed by those concrete fists again.

"Start talking." Cal crossed his arms.

"I owe you an apology, first of all." Deck didn't allow himself to look away from Cal's angry gaze. "Blaming you for Genie's death was unfair when it happened, and I'm sorry for not getting over it."

Cal's eyebrows rose, but he didn't say a word.

"Second," Deck went on. "I'm sorry for using your sister to make you pay. It was wrong and there's no excuse for it." He eyed the grim set of Cal's mouth. "And third, I'd like your permission to court your sister."

"What?" The word was an incredulous explosion. "You've already knocked her up; why in hell would you bother now?"

Deck didn't flinch. "If she'll forgive me, I want to marry her."

"And how are you going to manage that?"

Deck shrugged, heartened by the fact that Cal hadn't hauled off and slugged him yet. "I don't know yet."

Cal exhaled slowly. He put his hands on his hips and looked up, and his gaze followed the motions of a single red-tailed hawk drifting in the vast empty sky. "You *should* go on hating me," he said in a quiet voice. "If I hadn't been determined to show the world how tough I was that night, I wouldn't have needed a ride. Indirectly, I am responsible for Genie's death.'' He looked at Deck, and the torment in his gray eyes sent a shaft of guilt straight through Deck as he realized what Cal had lived with all these years. ''I'll probably always wonder why I didn't tell her to put on her seat belt.''

Deck drew in a sharp breath. ''You can't blame yourself for that.''

''Why not?'' His tone was bitter. ''You did.''

''I was wrong.'' Deck's voice vibrated with the intensity of his frustration. ''I blamed myself, too, you know. That's probably why I was so hard on you. It was easier than facing myself.''

''You didn't do anything to feel bad about.''

Deck snorted. ''No? Who was the first person you asked for a ride?''

A silence fell between the two men.

''You.'' It was little more than a hoarse whisper. ''My God, I'd forgotten.''

''I haven't.'' Deck took a deep breath. ''But Marty said something last night that made me realize how stupid it was to go on claiming blame for the rest of my life. I'm going to let go of it, starting today, and I'm releasing you, too.''

Another silence fell.

Cal's gaze met his across the distance between them. ''I guess this means I don't get to beat the tar out of you anymore.'' There was the faintest hint of the easiness they'd once shared.

Deck grinned, feeling better than he had in years. ''You don't get to *try,* you mean.'' He gestured to the truck. ''You going to town?''

''Yep.''

"Do you have any objections if I ride back to the house and talk to your sister?"

Cal's features tightened again. "I wouldn't, if she were there." He spread his hands. "I found a note on the table when I got home. She drove to Rapid last night."

"What'd she do that for?" Impatience swamped him, now that he was so close to having things back under control.

Cal's face was ashen beneath his newly acquired tan. "She flew home to Virginia this morning. She's already gone."

Already gone? He couldn't take it in, and he simply stood dumbly in the middle of the muddy lane.

"She was supposed to stay awhile longer, but she told me yesterday she had to leave. While I was in town last night, she left me a note and took off." Cal tipped his hat back and scratched his head. "What are you going to do?"

"I...don't know." He couldn't believe she'd left just like that, without a word to him. She was going to have *his baby,* dammit! How could she waltz off without even telling him? "Does she know you told me?"

"Nope. I haven't talked to her since then." Cal shook his head. "You going to go after her?"

Deck felt panicked. "I've never been East in my life."

"So you're going to forget her." Cal's voice was mild.

"Hell, no!" He reached for the trailing reins of his horse and swung himself into the saddle. "I guess I'm going to Virginia." He turned the gelding and urged him into a trot.

"Fly into D.C. or Richmond and catch a commuter flight to Charlottesville," Cal called after him. "You can rent a car from there."

She was pregnant. As he rushed back to the Lucky

Stryke, the memory of their last lovemaking preoccupied him. God, had it only been the night before last? It seemed like days. She'd been so warm and willing that he'd nearly forgotten the need for birth control. But when he'd reached for a condom she'd stopped him.

"No. You don't have to."

"Are you sure?"

"Positive."

And now he knew the meaning of the flicker of uncertainty that had flitted across her face. *Why hadn't she told him?*

Why would she, after what he'd done? If it weren't for the way she'd responded to him two nights ago, he'd have been sure she hated him. She might still, but if she did, why had she let him make love to her? And even more important, why had she melted against him and returned his embraces, his hot caresses and deep kisses, if she didn't care? Women didn't do that with a man they hated.

An hour later he was packed and explaining the whole crazy mess to Marty, when Cal's truck came roaring back the lane.

"Directions from the airport to the house." Cal passed him a piece of paper. "And before you go, there's something you should know." He grimaced. "A couple of somethings."

Deck shouldered his duffel bag and started out the door. "What?"

"Hold up. This is going to take a minute."

His tone of voice made Deck slow and turn. Setting a booted foot on the porch step, he lowered his duffel bag to the floor. "Okay. Talk."

Cal hesitated. "Did you know Silver was engaged a year ago back in Virginia?"

Engaged. A fist grabbed at his heart and squeezed painfully, and he actually raised a hand to massage his chest. "No, I didn't." A horrible thought occurred to him. "Is she still engaged?"

"No," Cal said hastily. "She ended it. But it wasn't pretty. He was a creep."

What did that mean? "Did he cheat on her?"

"No. But…"

"But *what?*"

"Silver's an heiress." Cal looked him square in the eye. "Didn't you know?"

An heiress. Money. Probably lots of money. "No. Hell, I didn't even know she was your sister, at first."

"Didn't see the family resemblance?" Cal turned to show off his profile.

"If she'd looked like you, she wouldn't have had to worry about a fiancé."

"Hmm. That didn't sound like a compliment. Guess you don't want to know the rest of the story."

Deck glanced at the watch he'd worn today. "Yeah, I do. Pronto. I've got a plane to catch."

The laughter faded from Cal's face. "Well, the short version is that when the guy found her money's tied up for a long time, he ditched her. She thought he loved her, and she was pretty broken up over it. And that's the other thing—her daddy is very protective. Silver's his only child. When he finds out what you've done, he's liable to give you an old-fashioned ass kicking."

Deck shouldered his duffel again. "Is that it?"

"It? You're going after a woman who's going to have a hell of a time trusting you again, *if* her daddy even lets you see her. Yeah." Cal nodded. "That's it."

"Thanks." Deck extended a hand and gave Cal's big paw a firm, grateful shake. Looking at his old friend, he added "I appreciate everything."

Nine

The mockingbird in the bush outside the window was making a terrible racket. Silver wondered if the neighbor's cat had stepped into the unofficial off-limits zone again. Yesterday, while she'd been sitting on the terrace, the bird had scared the fur right off that cat with his dive-bombing attacks. The funniest part about the whole thing was that the mockingbird's babies had left the nest the week before.

She couldn't even summon up the energy to laugh.

She opened her eyes. Above her was the familiar ceiling of the bedroom she'd lived in since she could remember, painted a particular shade of "candlelight" that her mother had ordered specially mixed by a decorator. Her room had matured as she had over the years, though the color scheme had changed little. The violets, sky-blues, pale-greens, creams and soft fabrics created a soothing effect enhanced by the light streaming through the French doors that led out onto a second-floor gallery running the length of the front of her family's antebellum home.

Her great-great-great-grandfather had built the home well before the Civil War not far from Jefferson's mountaintop estate, Monticello. It had been in her family through the generations and it would be hers someday.

And it would belong to her child someday as well.

As the pain slapped hard at her again, her breath caught in a soundless sob and she rolled over and buried her face in her pillow. She longed for Deck so desperately, nearly every minute of the day. He'd been so tender with her, so loving. Though he'd never mentioned love, she'd been sure he was planning their future together just as she was.

But he hadn't been. Willing the tears away, she flopped onto her back again and raised a hand. Protectively she rested her palm over her abdomen where her child was still hidden from the world.

Her child, not anyone else's. Deck had forfeited all rights to fatherhood when he'd deceived her so callously. A tiny twinge of guilt pricked at her conscience, though, and she defiantly dragged it out and confronted it.

Deck hadn't wanted her. She'd been only a means to an end. And a convenient sexual outlet. She had no obligation to give him any information about herself, and as far as she was concerned, this was something very personal about herself. He hadn't wanted her, she reminded herself again, and he wouldn't want her child.

Desperately, she forced herself to think about something else. Anything else. There was no reason in the world to waste any more of her brain cells on *him.*

Cal's phone call from the night before floated into her mind and she relaxed marginally. He was such a sweetie. Then her mood sank again as she recalled the direction of the conversation.

"How are you feeling?" he'd asked.

"Fine," she'd answered truthfully. She'd had no morning sickness to speak of.

"Are you going to stay in Charlottesville?"

"I haven't even thought about it." And she hadn't. "I suppose I might as well."

There was a silence. "Are you planning to tell—"

"No."

Another silence. "You sure? He might be sorry. He might want to—"

"You're crazy." Her voice was flat. "He hates your guts. Why are you defending him?"

"I'm not. But he *is* the father of your child."

"Biologically, yes. In any other respect that man is nothing—nothing!—to me or my child."

Cal had been smart enough to recognize the tone of a woman who wasn't going to be rational on a certain subject, and the talk had moved to less explosive topics. He had bought two hundred head of cattle and was hiring cowboys to work on the ranch. The remodeling project would be starting tomorrow, and he'd put up double sheets of plastic in the kitchen doorway to keep the worst of the mess out while the workmen were adding the rooms.

A rancher in the next county had gotten his pelvis smashed while trailing a herd to a new pasture. He'd been taking a break, sitting in the shade with a bunch of other cowboys drinking beer and telling stories while their horses grazed nearby. When a shadow fell over him, he'd looked up just in time to see the rump end of his horse coming down right on him.

"Nothing he could do," Cal had said. "When a horse decides to lie down, you don't want to be in the way."

"No kidding." She'd shaken her head ruefully, wondering how the man could have not noticed his horse getting so close.

So close…

Why was it that she believed, time and again, that she was so close to finding all she wanted in her life? Chet had swept her off her feet, flattering her, delighting her with little romantic touches that she'd never known before. Unlike Deck, who hadn't even bothered romancing her, Chet had spent a lot of time on the trappings of romance. She hadn't been hard to dazzle. She'd been a very naive young woman when she'd met him.

Her parents had kept her from forming any serious relationships at a younger age with their overprotectiveness. She'd gone to private girls-only academies throughout her educational years, up to and including college. And while she'd had a few fun little crushes during those years, she'd never felt that Mr. Right had knocked on the door to her heart.

Which was probably why she was such an easy mark for Chet. And Deck, she thought bitterly. Did she have a sign plastered on her back that read, "All I need is a little sweet talk?"

Things Deck had said and done had played and replayed themselves in her memory a thousand times on her trip home. She'd been home more than half a day, and the mental movies still ran relentlessly through her head.

"This is fate," and *"I have to do this,"* he'd said. She'd thought he meant she was irresistible, stupid as it seemed now. But all along, he'd had another agenda to follow. No wonder he'd been so determined to repair the rift between them after the night in her kitchen. He'd practically begged for another chance—not because he cared about her, but because he cared desperately about getting

close to her so he could hurt Cal. She was incidental to his thinking except for her usefulness in that respect.

And because she'd been easier to get into bed than a sleepy baby.

He hadn't even undressed completely that first time. She could feel her face flame at the memory of him still wearing his pants and boots. *Easy* wasn't even the appropriate word to use. She'd been a cakewalk. Why hadn't he just let it go after he'd accomplished his goal of seducing her?

Get real, girl. What man getting free sex is going to give it up voluntarily? The all-too-familiar prickle of tears burned at the backs of her eyes, and she got up restlessly, tossing off the covers and pacing around the beautiful prison of her room.

She hadn't gotten home until early evening. Her father had been waiting at the Charlottesville-Albemarle Airport, and they'd gone straight home, where her mother had been fussing over a supper of Virginia ham, green beans and yams, one of her favorites. They'd been surprised by her sudden appearance, but neither questioned it.

"Had enough of the Wild West?" her father had asked jovially. They'd cosseted and coddled her, and the minute she'd closed her door at bedtime she'd burst into tears, burying her face in the pillow to muffle the sounds.

She felt so guilty and ashamed. They were going to be so upset when she told them about her condition. For an instant she considered going away somewhere and bearing the child, then giving it up for adoption, but as quickly as the idea flitted into her head she rejected it. She could never give up her child. *Never.*

And Deck's child, a small inner voice reminded her. *A sweet, cooing blue-eyed baby with chestnut curls quirking all over his head....* The wave of pain was so fierce that she pressed her hands over her heart in an involuntary motion, but the hurt that sliced her wouldn't be stopped. She felt a howl bubbling to the surface of her forced calm, and she quickly raced into the bathroom and turned on the shower, then shed her nightgown and stood beneath the hot, driving spray while scalding tears slipped down her cheeks, and her body shook with the force of her sobs.

After the shower, she was so exhausted she nearly went back to bed, but instead she dressed in a loose-fitting, sleeveless denim dress that suited her lethargic mood and the steamy humidity of Virginia in June. Lyddie, the housekeeper who'd been with the family since before her birth, was on a high ladder dusting the chandelier that hung from the ceiling in the enormous foyer.

"Good morning, honey. Is it good to see you! I'm almost finished here. If you wait five minutes I'll fix you some breakfast."

Silver smiled and shook her head, waving at Lyddie to stay where she was. "No, you take your time. I can feed myself."

Though she wouldn't count herself spoiled, she'd always taken the immense wealth in her family for granted. Now, walking down the hall, she thought of the typical life-style in Kadoka. A maid would be as foreign to them as seeing a unicorn prancing across the prairie. She'd gotten accustomed to doing for herself while she was at Cal's, and she'd found that she liked it.

Now, with a baby on the way, she looked critically at her life-style. Did she want her child to grow up being waited on hand and foot as she had been? The answer was a quick and resounding No. Her childhood hadn't been horrible; far from it. And she didn't think she'd turned out so badly, even if her taste in men needed a major tune-up.

But she'd lived a fairy-tale life. She'd never skinned her knee, never tracked mud onto the kitchen floor, never fallen from anything she shouldn't have been climbing on in the first place and broken a bone. She'd spent all her time at home in white lacy socks, black patent leather Mary Janes and full skirts watching other children through the windows of her father's expensive European cars when he'd taken her somewhere. She'd played sedate games of dolls with the socially acceptable daughters of other moneyed families. She'd taken ballet, piano and riding lessons, and she'd gone through a finishing program, which included etiquette and ballroom dance classes with little boys in tuxedos and ruthlessly groomed hair who'd looked as though they'd rather be anywhere else on the planet.

The memory made her smile even as it reaffirmed her feelings about the way in which she would raise a child of her own.

A child of her own... That was her first order of business today, finding a doctor and having her first prenatal checkup. She sighed, remembering that she'd left South Dakota without keeping her doctor's appointment. Her family doctor here didn't do obstetrics. She'd have to figure out how to get a recommendation for a good obstetrician without everyone in her parents' social circle finding out that their daughter had gotten herself knocked up out West.

She winced. There was no way around it: she was going to have to tell her parents right away. Her mother would no doubt have the names of the best doctors in the area.

She put her dishes in the dishwasher and went back to her room to brush her teeth. A few minutes later, as she was looking up obstetricians in the Yellow Pages, the doorbell rang. Curious about who would be calling before nine in the morning, she came out of her room and leaned over the balcony rail as Lyddie bustled from the kitchen and went to the door. Her father came out of his office at one side of the foyer and leaned against the door frame.

When the door swung open, the first thing she saw from her vantage point was the crown of a black Stetson. Though his face was shaded from above, she'd recognize that long, lean body anywhere, and she reeled back against the wall in absolute, utter shock, one hand flying to her mouth to stifle the exclamation that nearly escaped.

Deck!

"Mrs. Jenssen?" Deck offered his right hand.

"No, I'm the maid. I'll go and get her." Lyddie started to turn, but Deck reached out and touched her arm.

"No, wait. Actually I've come to talk to Silver."

Her father straightened from his slouch and approached the door. "I'll take care of this," he said to Lyddie. As the maid went down the hallway to the kitchen, Deck offered her father his hand. "Mr. Jenssen? I'm Deck Stryker."

Her father reached slowly for Deck's hand, a puzzled look on his face. He clearly was wondering if he should recognize the cowboy standing before him. She was sure he had no idea what this man was doing at his door at— she glanced at her watch—eight-thirty on a weekday morning.

"May I help you, Mr. Stryker?"

"I'd like to speak to Silver."

"Does she know you?" Her father was rallying.

"Yes. I live on the ranch next to her brother's in South Dakota."

"You've come a long way." Her father sounded mystified. He turned and went to the intercom but before he could use it, she stepped forward and spoke over the railing. "I'm here, Daddy."

Her father and Deck both looked up. Purposely she kept her gaze on her father's face as he indicated Deck with a wave of his hand. "This gentleman's come to speak to you, dear. What shall I tell him?"

She nearly laughed aloud. Deck was no one's idea of a gentleman! And she could tell him herself—she was standing right there. She started down the stairs, addressing Deck directly. "I don't have anything to say to you." But her voice faltered into silence as her eyes met his stormy blue ones.

"Oh, I believe you do," he said, and there was a bite to the words that made her father straighten in alarm.

"Mr. Stryker—"

"Call me Deck." He moved easily around her father to the foot of the stairs as she came to the bottom, and she stopped one step up, unwilling to get too close to him. It brought her eyes on a level with the grim line of his mouth. "Were you running out on me?" he murmured to her.

"Hardly." She made her voice cool and reasonable though every nerve in her body was jangling a nervous alarm at his proximity. "I have a life here. It was time to get back."

"You could have a life there, too."

"It was time to get back," she repeated. She didn't understand his cryptic words, and she had no intention of asking him what he meant.

Deck gave her a level look. "And it didn't occur to you that it might be nice of you to let me know you were thinking of leaving?"

She shrugged, looking away from him as if the conversation was merely a polite exchange between acquaintances. "We were only casual—"

His hand shot out and gripped her chin before she could think to evade him, startling her and forcing her to look at him. Lightning bolts shot from his eyes, silencing her as she automatically put up her hand and circled his thick wrist. "There was nothing casual about us and you know it, you little liar." Deck's veneer of civility was thin; the words were a snarl.

"Now look here, Stryker." Her father stepped forward. "I'm going to have to ask you to take your hands off my daughter and leave the premises." He paused, and when Deck completely ignored him, he went on. "Or I'll be forced to call the police."

"Cal told me," Deck said to her, still ignoring her father. His fingers gentled on her chin, sliding up to cup her cheek. Then his sapphire gaze sharpened as he surveyed her face. "You've been crying," he stated. "Why?"

Another wave of shock rolled through her at his first words; she barely heard the question. *Cal had told him she was pregnant?* It rattled her badly for a moment, but she forced herself to keep breathing and not drop her gaze from his. She didn't believe him. After the way the two men had acted toward each other the one and only time she'd ever seen them sharing the same space, she sincerely doubted Cal had told him *that*.

"Cal told you what?" She straightened and turned her head away from the scorching touch of his fingers on her face, releasing her grip on his arm and stepping past him into the foyer, forcing herself to ignore the butterflies fluttering in her stomach at the simple pleasure of being so close to his strong, hard body again. "It's all right, Daddy. Deck will be leaving in a minute."

"Deck will not be leaving in a minute," he said from

behind her through what sounded suspiciously like gritted teeth. "Deck won't be going anywhere until Silver is packed and ready to go with him."

"What?" Silver and her father both spoke at the same time.

She recovered first. "I'm not going anywhere with you. I owe you *nothing*."

Her father, apparently realizing that this was something more than a simple visit from an unwelcome suitor, said nothing further.

"Have you told him?" Deck jerked his head in her father's direction.

"I haven't told him anything."

"Amen to that," muttered her father.

"There's nothing to tell," she went on. "I don't know why you traveled all this way. You've wasted your time. I'm not planning any more visits to Kadoka."

"I'm sorry to hear that, since all these trees and hills are making me claustrophobic as hell," Deck said. "But I guess if you really want to live here, I'll find something to do."

"Now wait a minute." Her father suddenly came to life. "Silver may be an heiress but before this goes any further you need to know that her money's tied up in trust." His voice was triumphant. "You'll never see a single penny of her millions."

For the first time, Deck appeared taken aback. "Millions? She's worth millions?"

"Yes, but don't—"

"Keep them. I don't care if she doesn't have a penny to her name, I still want her, and I want our child. I can't give her millions but we'll live comfortably."

There was a stunned silence as his words echoed off the flagstone flooring in the big space.

Silver dropped her head and covered her face with her hands. "Cal *did* tell you. That creep."

"He's not a creep. He loves you."

Her father cleared his throat. "Silver, are you—"

"Since when are you and Cal such good buddies that you champion each other? He killed your sister, remember?" Her angry words overrode her father's voice. It was a petty, vicious thing to say, but he'd caught her off guard and she was feeling far too vulnerable.

"This sounds like an entirely too complicated problem to unravel standing here," her father declared firmly. He turned to Deck. "Would you like to come in, Mr. Stryker, and continue this discussion?"

"No!"

"Yes." Deck ignored her protest. "Thank you, sir."

Silver turned on her father, ready to give him her opinion of his meddling but the expression in his eyes stopped her before a word slipped out.

"Are you pregnant?" he asked quietly.

She wanted to lie, to deny it, to send Deck away so she could cry as she so desperately wanted to do, but that was no longer an option. "Yes." She didn't dare look at Deck, and she couldn't meet her father's eyes. "I'm sorry, Daddy. I didn't want you to find out like this. I was planning to tell you soon."

Her father indicated the hallway leading back to the family room. "Why don't we make ourselves more comfortable and talk about this?"

"If you don't mind, I believe Silver and I need to speak privately," Deck told him.

Her father nodded slowly. "Of course." He inclined his head toward his office. "I'll be working if you need me," he said to Silver. He hesitated, then addressed Deck one final time. "My daughter will receive my full support in whatever decision she makes, but I meant what I said about the money.''

''So did I.'' Deck's voice was level, but anger licked at the edges of his words. ''You can keep every damn dollar you have. All I want is your daughter.''

Her father nodded. But as he turned toward his office, Silver caught a faint smile curling the corners of his lips.

Deck was watching her the way she imagined a predator might watch its cornered prey. But when he spoke, his tone was mild. ''Let's sit down somewhere and talk.''

She sighed. If she knew anything about him, it was that he wouldn't go away until he'd had his say. She might as well get this over with and then she could ship him back to the Badlands where he belonged.

Silently she led the way down the hallway and into the family's informal living room. Taking a seat in a chair, she indicated that he should do the same. He ignored her, walking across the room to stand with his back to her, gazing out through the French doors to the elegant patio beyond.

''Would you care for a drink?'' She would be civilized if it killed her.

''No.'' He turned to face her. ''Why didn't you tell me you were pregnant?''

''I—'' She swallowed.

''You knew the other night.'' It wasn't a question.

She didn't pretend not to know what he was talking about. ''Yes, I knew.'' She looked at him, seeing the way his tall figure blocked the light from the window, the foreign look that he gave the home of her childhood, with his black hat and scuffed boots and mile-wide shoulders. ''I didn't think it would matter to you.''

''You didn't think— Good God, woman, what kind of man do you think I am, that I wouldn't want to know about my own child?'' The words were ripped from his throat, and for the first time she saw the raw fury that he'd held in check.

It took everything she had in her not to shrink from the angry blue eyes boring into her, but she stiffened her spine and spoke again. ''You were so consumed with hate that there wasn't room for anything else in your life. What was I supposed to think?''

His shoulders slumped, and she realized her words had hit a vulnerable spot. ''You're right,'' he said more quietly. ''I treated you badly. And I'm sorry for it.''

''Yes, you did.'' He was looking for an absolution that she couldn't offer.

''Silver.'' Deck covered the space between them and reached for her, cupping her elbows and drawing her to her feet. ''I want you to marry me.''

''Marry you?'' She recoiled. It took her a long moment to marshal enough words to form another coherent thought. Despite everything, her heart leaped high and began to pound fiercely within her. A stern order to herself to settle down was useless. Then hurt and anger began to seep back into her mind with the returning memories. ''The altitude in these mountains must be affecting your brain. Go back to Kadoka and wallow in the success of your revenge.''

''I can't.'' His words were quiet.

''Why not?'' The raw pain that slashed her heart apart nearly brought her to her knees and she wrapped her arms around herself tightly as if to stave off further hurt. ''You were pretty pleased with yourself when you threw our— *your* successful seduction in my brother's face.''

''Our lovemaking,'' he corrected her.

''It wasn't lovemaking. It was me thinking we were

creating something special and you thinking you'd found the perfect way to make Cal pay.''

"It wasn't like that," he said grimly. "I'd been worrying for days about how to work it out. Cal coming home early really screwed things up, and I was wrong not to fix the years of bad feelings right then and there."

"You weren't wrong. It all worked out exactly like you planned."

"Except that you got hurt."

"If that was a concern, you should have thought of it before." Tears were starting to slip from her eyes now, and she angrily dashed them away. "Get out of here. You heard my father. He'll never give you any money if I marry you."

His jaw tightened. "I didn't even know your family *had* money until Cal told me. He can keep his money. I only want you."

"You want this baby," she corrected. "If you hadn't found out I was pregnant, you'd be riding around on your precious prairie right now. I'd be the last thing on your mind."

"You know better than that." Frustration colored his tone.

"Do I?" She threw down the gauntlet. "I've been lied to before. I don't intend to be so stupid a second time."

There was a silence as he digested her words. His face darkened as he realized she really didn't believe him. "I'm not your ex-boyfriend," he said.

"No, you aren't." She turned away and sat on the edge of the love seat, suddenly too weary to continue the argument. "Deck, I can't do this. I can't—"

"You don't have to." Before she could evade him, he was behind her, his big body warm against her as he put his arms around her and drew her back to lie against his broad chest. "Let me take care of you, honey. Marry me and let me worry about everything."

She lay against him, listening to the steady beat of his heart beneath her ear, her body warming to the touch of his hands on her even as she resisted relaxing into the comforting embrace. "How can I trust you?" she whispered in an anguished voice.

His arms tightened around her. "I can't answer that one. All I can do is promise you that after we're married you and the baby will be the most important things in my life."

She was silent, her mind a swimming jumble of disconnected thoughts. She loved him so much. Having his arms around her again, trying not to think of his offer of marriage, she thought that this must be her personal punishment for all the bad things she'd ever done in her entire life.

Could she marry him knowing that he didn't love her? He made no bones about his interest in the baby—she'd be playing second fiddle to this child and others that came along in the years to come. It wasn't supposed to be like that. Could she do it?

She froze as she realized what she was thinking. *More* children? She could see them learning to ride as they learned to walk, children who looked like Marty's beautiful little charmer, Cheyenne.

She didn't want to be married for the child she carried any more than she'd wanted to be married for the money that came with her family name. But as she looked into the days and weeks and years of the future, she couldn't see another man ever taking Deck's place in her heart. Would it be enough to share his life and his children, to know that he would never love her the way she wanted, *needed* him to?

The answer, when she set aside her wounded pride and her feelings of betrayal, was simple. She'd rather live with him than without him. Period. No matter that she wasn't the most important thing in his life. She would have part of him, a vital part, and they would share something special and irreplaceable in the family they would create together.

"All right," she said quietly. "I'll marry you."

His muscles bunched as her words penetrated, and she thought he held his breath for a moment. Then his big frame relaxed again, and the arms around her tightened. He bent his head and kissed her temple. "You won't regret it. I promise."

Then his hands slipped to her waist, lifting and turning her until she lay across his lap, her head cradled in one of his arms. He bent his head to hers, muttering, "I went crazy when I found out you were gone. Don't ever do that to me again."

And as Silver opened her mouth beneath his purposeful kiss, her heart shattered into even smaller pieces. His words were bittersweet, because she knew the only reason he'd gotten so frantic was because he'd learned she carried his child.

Ten

She was too quiet. Ever since she'd agreed to marry him she'd been like this, he thought. It was nothing he could put his finger on, exactly, nothing he could pinpoint. But Silver lacked some vital spark that she'd had before.

Was she having second thoughts? Deck had to admit that if he were Silver he'd think twice about giving up the obvious wealth her father had. Although the Stryker outfit did well, he would never be able to give her the things her family could...the things that the "right" kind of socially acceptable man could. Was she sorry she'd be losing all that?

He sure as hell hoped not, because there was no way he was letting her go. He hadn't come after her only to lose her again. He was pretty sure she loved him, pretty sure that even if she hadn't loved him the first time he'd made love to her, she'd fallen in love with him soon after. A woman couldn't fake something like that. Could she?

She'd thought for a long time before she'd finally agreed to marry him, and he'd wondered what was going on behind those beautiful eyes of hers. As the silence had stretched without an answer, he'd been halfway to panic for fear she would refuse.

Right now another pair of eyes as beautiful as Silver's were assessing him with frank thoroughness across the dining room table. Silver's mother—and Cal's mother, too, he thought—had invited him to come to dinner that same evening after Silver had broken the news of their impending marriage and parenthood to her parents. Her father had offered surprisingly little resistance, though Deck was sure the man considered him little more than another opportunistic gold digger out for his daughter's inheritance. Well, time would take care of that misconception, so he wasn't going to worry about it.

What he *was* worried about was Mrs. Jenssen. Silver obviously cared a great deal for her parents; their opinions would be important to her. And though she certainly knew him well enough to discount her father's fears, she might listen to a mother who didn't consider him a suitable husband. After all, this was the woman who'd hated life on the prairie so much she'd left behind her husband and infant son when she'd decided to leave and go back East. No, he wasn't going to feel comfortable until Silver wore his ring on her finger and he had her back in South Dakota with him where she belonged.

"So, Mr. Stryker, tell us about your ranch. I remember your mother, but I didn't live in South Dakota long enough to make many lasting memories." Mrs. Jenssen took a bite of her meal, set down her fork and folded her hands in her lap, looking at him in inquiry. Hell. He'd never liked being the center of attention. This was going to be one long damned meal.

"My brother and I run an Angus cow-calf outfit in southwestern South Dakota. We're on the edge of the Badlands, about an hour from the eastern edge of the Black Hills." He paused, but Silver's parents waited expectantly. "There's plenty of room for two families on the land. Silver and I will probably build our own place."

Silver tilted her head at that, and her eyebrows rose. He realized they hadn't even discussed elementary issues like where they'd live, and he shut his mouth with a snap. He was done explaining things.

"Silver hasn't told us how you met," said her father.

Great. He guessed he wasn't done explaining. But before he could begin to tell her parents what he'd done, Silver stepped into the silence. "Deck and his brother grew up with Cal. Cal's ranch adjoins Deck's." She smiled across the corner of the table at him, and he wondered if he was the only one who could see the shadows clouding her bright eyes. "Actually, we ran into each other in the literal sense in the grocery store the first time we met."

Silver stopped speaking, and her parents both nodded, apparently satisfied with her brief version of events. He cleared his throat and reached across the table, determined to erase those shadows in her eyes. "I knew the moment I saw her that I wanted her to be mine."

But her eyes didn't lighten. Instead she dropped her gaze to her plate. If he didn't know better, he would think he'd embarrassed her.

"Well." Her mother daintily dabbed her napkin at the corners of the perfect lipstick on her lips. "Have you decided on a date for the wedding? There's a lot to do in a short amount of time. I'll have to contact the caterer, the florist and find some suitable musicians. Invitations will have to go out this week. We can have the reception here.

I suppose we could even have the wedding here if we can't find an appropriate church. I wonder if there'd be any chance that the university chapel would be free on a Saturday or even a Sunday.... I'll call over there and find out—''

"Mother. We don't want a big wedding." Silver spoke quietly but he detected a note of desperation in her voice. It matched the way he felt at the prospect of a huge formal affair like the one her mother obviously had in mind.

"Of course not, dear, given the circumstances. We should be able to keep it under one hundred and fifty. Will anyone from your family attend?" She looked expectantly at Deck.

"No, Mother. You don't understand." Silver clutched his hand, her fingers digging painfully into his palm. "Not a hundred and fifty. Not even fifty. No elaborate plans, no reception. We could even be married at the courthouse."

At the courthouse? He wasn't thrilled at the thought of a fancy wedding, but the idea of a civil ceremony didn't sit well. He turned to her mother, whose mouth was opening and closing soundlessly, quickly jumping into the breach before the woman could get wound up again. "Silver and I need to talk about this before we make any plans. Excuse us."

Surging to his feet, he kept his grip on Silver's hand. She rose, still avoiding his eyes, and allowed him to lead her toward the kitchen door. He towed her through the kitchen, nodding to Lyddie, the maid—the *maid,* for God's sake—and moved right on out to the steps that led off the patio into a quaint little formal rose garden. At least the gardener wasn't around. There was a small stone bench at the far end, and he took her to it, pulling her down beside him. "All right, talk."

For the first time since he'd told her parents he'd wanted her, she met his eyes. "What is there to say?"

He nearly exploded. "How the hell should I know? You've been acting funny the whole day since you agreed to marry me. Is it that terrible a prospect?"

"I'm facing some momentous changes in my life," she said with quiet dignity. She linked her fingers together in her lap, and he could see the tension in her tight grip. "Marriage, motherhood, moving halfway across the country…"

He heard the quaver in her voice, and he'd never felt more helpless in his whole life. Because of him, she was dealing with all of those things. At once.

Not knowing what else to do, he put his arms around her and drew her to him, resting his cheek against her silky hair. "You don't have to do any of those things alone. This marriage is going to be a partnership all the way." He was distracted by the light, gentle fragrance that emanated from her warm body, the softness of her curves beneath his hands, and he slid his palms up and down her back soothingly, enjoying the contact.

"Deck—" She hesitated, then drew back from his caressing hands. "I'm not sure this is a good idea. I know you want to be a father to your child, but marriage is a big step—"

Panic rose up and grabbed him by the throat faster than the words could leave her mouth. He gripped both her upper arms and held her so she couldn't walk away from him. "We're getting married. Period."

"No." She shook her head, and he could see tears pooling in her eyes. "I don't think we are."

"Why not?" he demanded, and he could hear the panic in his voice. "I already told you that if you can't live out

West we can stay here. And I know you love me, so that's not the problem.''

''But that's exactly the problem.'' She wrenched herself away from him and scrambled to her feet, and the tears she'd been fighting made silver rivers down her cheeks. Her voice trembled and broke. ''I know you want me now, but what happens when the sex isn't enough? You won't always feel like this about me. What will happen then?''

He stared at her, wondering what in hell she was talking about. His stomach twisted into a tight knot at the thought of losing her; she *had* to marry him. ''Of course I'll always feel like this about you. Why wouldn't I?''

She raised a hand and swiped a tear from her cheek, her agitation visible. ''Oh, don't be so dense! I'm *not* going to be pretty about seven months from now when I resemble a hippo more than a woman. And eventually I'm going to age. Wrinkles, stretch marks maybe, gray hair.'' She made wild gestures with her hands, and he rose, snagging her flailing fists and holding her still.

''Will you still love me when I go gray?'' he asked.

She gazed up at him blankly. Then she said quietly, ''The way I feel about you isn't going to change with age.''

''Exactly.'' He drew her in and pinned her against his chest when she would have struggled away. ''So why do you think I'll love you any less?''

''I—what?'' She stopped struggling and went dead still beneath his hands. The color left her face, and he had a serious moment of fear that she was going to faint right in front of him.

And then it hit him.

She'd been his since the first time he'd seen her. And once they'd made love, she'd worn her feelings on her sleeve. Though she hadn't said it aloud until this evening, he'd known she loved him, had accepted the precious gift without a second thought. He'd been so sure of her love that he'd hopped on a plane for the first time in his life and come after her, even though he'd taken her heart and trampled it beneath his heel only days before.

No wonder she didn't think he loved her! What had he done to let her know how much she meant to him? He wasn't big on romantic gestures, hadn't ever spent a moment reassuring her the way he knew women needed. Remorse peppered his conscience with relentless force.

He still was holding her between his hands and she still was staring at him as if he'd grown a third eye. Gently he slipped his hands from her arms up to cup her shoulders.

"I said I love you," he told her. "I've never been good with words, and I should have told you before. I will love you for the rest of my life. *Our* lives," he amended. "Why the hell else would I offer to live here if I didn't?" He drew her close, wrapping his arms around her and aligning her body with his in the familiar position that made her purr deep in her throat. "Now will you please *marry* me?"

She slid her arms around his neck as her face began to glow, and he watched the sparkle come back into the eyes he'd been unable to forget since their very first meeting. "I'd be happy to marry you," she said with a catch in her voice. "Will you say it again?"

"I love you." He grinned, feeling like hooting and hollering and imagining her mother's shocked reaction if he did. "I wouldn't mind hearing it, either."

She looked startled. "You know I love you. Don't you?" She blushed. "After the way I was with you…didn't you know?"

"I was pretty sure." He shrugged. "But it's nice to know for sure." He bent his head and found her lips, murmuring against her mouth, "No more tears, now. We have something better to do." Then he tore himself away from the kiss that threatened to flame out of control, looking over her head at the big house with its wide windows at the far end of the yard. "Is there any place on this property where we can't be seen from those damned windows?"

Silver laughed aloud as she slipped from his arms and drew him farther into the garden. "I imagine we can find something if we look hard enough."

Two weeks later Deck moved into position at the altar of the little stone chapel on the campus of the University of Virginia. The strains of some lilting piece of music swelled as Cal took his place beside him and they watched one of Silver's cousins make her way to the altar at a measured pace.

Silver's mother had compromised, and the guest list had numbered less than fifty, all immediate family. And all hers, since his couldn't be there. But he'd refused to wait any longer than two weeks, and when she realized he was serious about flying back to South Dakota and marrying there, Mrs. Jenssen had stopped cajoling and started planning.

A motion at the rear of the church caught his eye, and he looked back to see his bride coming toward him on her father's arm.

She was so beautiful he couldn't believe she was going to be his. Her gown was simple, baring her smooth ivory shoulders and brushing the floor with each step she took. Around her neck she wore her mother's pearls and in her ears were the pearl-and-diamond drops he'd given her the night before. She glowed with a special inner light that came from either love or pregnancy, he wasn't sure which.

Thinking of the night before made his mind leap ahead to the night to come. The past two weeks had dragged. He'd gone back to South Dakota after agreeing upon the details of the wedding and the date of the ceremony, working with Marty to get the ranch in shape so that he could take some time for a honeymoon in a few weeks.

He'd come back East yesterday for the wedding rehearsal, bringing Cal along to be his best man, since both he and Marty couldn't leave the ranch at the same time. When she'd realized that he and her brother had truly reconciled their differences, Silver had been visibly touched and openly thrilled.

He was less exuberant, but he felt pleased with the peace that had settled into his mind since he'd let go of his misplaced anger and self-hatred. His anguish over Genie's death had gentled, as well, to aching regret and sad acceptance. And there was another balm to soothe his heart, as he thought of Lyn. He'd played a part in saving her life, and she was doing well. Silver had conned Cal into hiring her as his housekeeper and she would be staying at his ranch once the doctors felt she was strong enough to resume normal activities.

And as his silver-eyed bride, the instrument of his salvation from himself, left her father and took his hand before the minister, he knew he owed his peace of mind to her. Silver had come into his life and forced him to confront himself. She'd healed the raw places inside him and filled every corner of his being with her love—a love that would be his for the rest of his life.

He turned to speak his vows and had to clear his throat on a sudden surge of emotion, and Silver looked up at him and smiled. In her shining face he saw his future, and he held her gaze with his as he began their life together.

"I, George Deckett Stryker, take you, Silver Anne Jenssen, to be my wife..."

*   *   *   *   *

If you enjoyed what you just read,
then we've got an offer you can't resist!

Take 2 bestselling
love stories FREE!
Plus get a FREE surprise gift!

///////////////////////////////

Clip this page and mail it to Silhouette Reader Service™

IN U.S.A.	**IN CANADA**
3010 Walden Ave.	P.O. Box 609
P.O. Box 1867	Fort Erie, Ontario
Buffalo, N.Y. 14240-1867	L2A 5X3

YES! Please send me 2 free Silhouette Desire® novels and my free surprise gift. Then send me 6 brand-new novels every month, which I will receive months before they're available in stores. In the U.S.A., bill me at the bargain price of $3.34 plus 25¢ delivery per book and applicable sales tax, if any*. In Canada, bill me at the bargain price of $3.74 plus 25¢ delivery per book and applicable taxes**. That's the complete price and a savings of at least 10% off the cover prices—what a great deal! I understand that accepting the 2 free books and gift places me under no obligation ever to buy any books. I can always return a shipment and cancel at any time. Even if I never buy another book from Silhouette, the 2 free books and gift are mine to keep forever. So why not take us up on our invitation. You'll be glad you did!

225 SEN C222
326 SEN C223

Name _____ (PLEASE PRINT)

Address _____ Apt.#

City _____ State/Prov. _____ Zip/Postal Code

* Terms and prices subject to change without notice. Sales tax applicable in N.Y.
** Canadian residents will be charged applicable provincial taxes and GST.
   All orders subject to approval. Offer limited to one per household.
   ® are registered trademarks of Harlequin Enterprises Limited.

DES00   ©1998 Harlequin Enterprises Limited

SILHOUETTE'S 20TH ANNIVERSARY CONTEST
OFFICIAL RULES
NO PURCHASE NECESSARY TO ENTER

1. To enter, follow directions published in the offer to which you are responding. Contest begins 1/1/00 and ends on 8/24/00 (the "Promotion Period"). Method of entry may vary. Mailed entries must be postmarked by 8/24/00, and received by 8/31/00.

2. During the Promotion Period, the Contest may be presented via the Internet. Entry via the Internet may be restricted to residents of certain geographic areas that are disclosed on the Web site. To enter via the Internet, if you are a resident of a geographic area in which Internet entry is permissible, follow the directions displayed on-line, including typing your essay of 100 words or fewer telling us "Where In The World Your Love Will Come Alive." On-line entries must be received by 11:59 p.m. Eastern Standard time on 8/24/00. Limit one e-mail entry per person, household and e-mail address per day, per presentation. If you are a resident of a geographic area in which entry via the Internet is permissible, you may, in lieu of submitting an entry on-line, enter by mail, by hand-printing your name, address, telephone number and contest number/name on an 8"x 11" plain piece of paper and telling us in 100 words or fewer "Where In The World Your Love Will Come Alive," and mailing via first-class mail to: Silhouette 20th Anniversary Contest, (in the U.S.) P.O. Box 9069, Buffalo, NY 14269-9069; (In Canada) P.O. Box 637, Fort Erie, Ontario, Canada L2A 5X3. Limit one 8"x 11" mailed entry per person, household and e-mail address per day. <u>On-line and/or 8"x 11" mailed entries received from persons residing in geographic areas in which Internet entry is not permissible will be disqualified.</u> No liability is assumed for lost, late, incomplete, inaccurate, nondelivered or misdirected mail, or misdirected e-mail, for technical, hardware or software failures of any kind, lost or unavailable network connection, or failed, incomplete, garbled or delayed computer transmission or any human error which may occur in the receipt or processing of the entries in the contest.

3. Essays will be judged by a panel of members of the Silhouette editorial and marketing staff based on the following criteria:

   Sincerity (believability, credibility)—50%

   Originality (freshness, creativity)—30%

   Aptness (appropriateness to contest ideas)—20%

   Purchase or acceptance of a product offer does not improve your chances of winning. In the event of a tie, duplicate prizes will be awarded.

4. All entries become the property of Harlequin Enterprises Ltd., and will not be returned. Winner will be determined no later than 10/31/00 and will be notified by mail. Grand Prize winner will be required to sign and return Affidavit of Eligibility within 15 days of receipt of notification. Noncompliance within the time period may result in disqualification and an alternative winner may be selected. All municipal, provincial, federal, state and local laws and regulations apply. Contest open only to residents of the U.S. and Canada who are 18 years of age or older, and is void wherever prohibited by law. Internet entry is restricted solely to residents of those geographical areas in which Internet entry is permissible. Employees of Torstar Corp., their affiliates, agents and members of their immediate families are not eligible. Taxes on the prizes are the sole responsibility of winners. Entry and acceptance of any prize offered constitutes permission to use winner's name, photograph or other likeness for the purposes of advertising, trade and promotion on behalf of Torstar Corp. without further compensation to the winner, unless prohibited by law. Torstar Corp and D.L. Blair, Inc., their parents, affiliates and subsidiaries, are not responsible for errors in printing or electronic presentation of contest or entries. In the event of printing or other errors which may result in unintended prize values or duplication of prizes, all affected contest materials or entries shall be null and void. If for any reason the Internet portion of the contest is not capable of running as planned, including infection by computer virus, bugs, tampering, unauthorized intervention, fraud, technical failures, or any other causes beyond the control of Torstar Corp. which corrupt or affect the administration, secrecy, fairness, integrity or proper conduct of the contest, Torstar Corp. reserves the right, at its sole discretion, to disqualify any individual who tampers with the entry process and to cancel, terminate, modify or suspend the contest or the Internet portion thereof. In the event of a dispute regarding an on-line entry, the entry will be deemed submitted by the authorized holder of the e-mail account submitted at the time of entry. Authorized account holder is defined as the natural person who is assigned to an e-mail address by an Internet access provider, on-line service provider or other organization that is responsible for arranging e-mail address for the domain associated with the submitted e-mail address.

5. Prizes: Grand Prize—a $10,000 vacation to anywhere in the world. Travelers (at least one must be 18 years of age or older) or parent or guardian if one traveler is a minor, must sign and return a Release of Liability prior to departure. Travel must be completed by December 31, 2001, and is subject to space and accommodations availability. Two hundred (200) Second Prizes—a two-book limited edition autographed collector set from one of the Silhouette Anniversary authors: Nora Roberts, Diana Palmer, Linda Howard or Annette Broadrick (value $10.00 each set). All prizes are valued in U.S. dollars.

6. For a list of winners (available after 10/31/00), send a self-addressed, stamped envelope to: Harlequin Silhouette 20th Anniversary Winners, P.O. Box 4200, Blair, NE 68009-4200.

Contest sponsored by Torstar Corp., P.O. Box 9042, Buffalo, NY 14269-9042.

ENTER FOR A CHANCE TO WIN*

Silhouette's 20th Anniversary Contest

Tell Us Where in the World You Would Like *Your* Love To Come Alive... And We'll Send the Lucky Winner There!

Silhouette wants to take you wherever your happy ending can come true.

Here's how to enter: Tell us, in 100 words or less, where you want to go to make your love come alive!

In addition to the grand prize, there will be 200 runner-up prizes, collector's-edition book sets autographed by one of the Silhouette anniversary authors: **Nora Roberts, Diana Palmer, Linda Howard** or **Annette Broadrick**.

DON'T MISS YOUR CHANCE TO WIN! ENTER NOW! No Purchase Necessary

Silhouette®
Where love comes alive™

Visit Silhouette at www.eHarlequin.com to enter, starting this summer.

Name: _____

Address: _____

City: _____ State/Province: _____

Zip/Postal Code: _____

Mail to Harlequin Books: **In the U.S.**: P.O. Box 9069, Buffalo, NY 14269-9069; **In Canada**: P.O. Box 637, Fort Erie, Ontario, L4A 5X3